I0666448

WHAT COMES AROUND

A quirky, touching, and unique novel of a gay man's quest to find a meaningful relationship. Written over a period of twenty-five years, these fifteen linked short stories—many of which have appeared in literary magazines and anthologies—exploit the narrator's heightened wit and self-examination by utilizing a second person point of view technique. Covering four decades of misadventures of looking for the right man, Currier's unnamed narrator bumps through blind dates, break-ups, unexpected seductions, tragedies, and imperfect affairs. Currier was awarded a New York Foundation for the Arts fellowship for the stories included in *What Comes Around*.

"Currier is adept at drawing a fine line between the erotic and the tragic, and at telling stories that 'although personal, are also the stories of our community.'"
—*The New York Times Book Review*

"Jameson Currier's kind of fiction can recreate reality more accurately than a cinema verité account of our daily lives."
—*The Washington Post Book World*

Jameson Currier is the author of four novels: *Where the Rainbow Ends*, *The Wolf at the Door*, *What Comes Around*, and *The Third Buddha*; and four collections of short fiction: *Dancing on the Moon*; *Desire, Lust, Passion, Sex*; *Still Dancing: New and Selected Stories*; and *The Haunted Heart and Other Tales*.

Also by Jameson Currier

WHAT COMES AROUND

a novel

JAMESON CURRIER

Chelsea Station Editions

New York

What Comes Around
by Jameson Currier

Book design by Peachboy Distillery & Designs
Cover art by Peachboy Distillery & Designs from a photo by Sergiy Chmara/ Shutterstock

Published by Chelsea Station Editions
362 West 36th Street, Suite 2R
New York, NY 10018
www.chelseastationeditions.com
info@chelseastationeditions.com

ISBN: 978-1-937627-05-8
Library of Congress Control Number: 2012951541

"What You Learn" was published in *Best Gay Erotica 2004* and originally appeared in *Absinthe Literary Review* and *OutsiderInk*. "What You Pay" was first published in *Rainbow Curve*. "What Counts Most" was originally published in *Boyfriends from Hell*. An earlier version of "What You Talk About" was first published in *Christopher Street, Dancing on the Moon,* and *Still Dancing.* "What is Enough?" was published in *Best Gay Erotica 1998* and originally appeared as "What You Think About" in *The Great Lawn.* "What You Feel" was first published in *Ex-Lover Weird Shit.* "What Does It Take?" was first published in *Wet Dreams, Wet Nightmares.* "What You Find" was first published in *The Unmade Bed: Twentieth Century Erotica* and in *Velvet Mafia.* "What You Save" was first published as "Drownings" in *580 Split.* "What You Learn," "What You Find," "What Counts Most," and What is Enough?" were also published in the author's collection *Desire, Lust, Passion, Sex* (Green Candy Press, 2004).

Grateful acknowledgment is made to the New York Foundation of the Arts for its generous support.

Contents

What You Learn

You are fifteen years old. It is summer; school is out. Your father is letting you drive to the pool. He mentions a stop sign you are approaching and you tap the brake pedal to begin stopping. The car has power brakes. It lurches with your tap, lurches again when you release the pedal. You let out a giggle. Your father tells you not to be so nervous and to turn on the left turn signal. You feel a bit of sweat beneath your arms and on your forehead. You think about turning down the radio and turning up the air conditioner but there is too much to think about already in front of you. You are glad when you finally reach the country club.

Your father tells you to park away from the other cars. He points to a spot that makes you turn your head. You turn the wheel at the same time. You almost cause a collision with a passing car but you right the wheel at the last possible moment. Blood has drained from your dad's face. He doesn't speak as you lurch the car to a stop. Then, when you have turned the ignition off, he says, "I'll meet you back here after your class."

Inside the club, you sign in and walk back outside to the pool area to join the other guys who are taking the class. Lifeguard Certification. Three hours every weekday for two weeks. Your father thinks it will help you get a summer job. He thinks you can be a lifeguard at the country club. Your dad was an Eagle Scout when he was a teenager. Your older brother is a football player. Your dad thinks you need to stop reading so many books and get outside more often. The swimming class was his idea, not yours.

Outside it is bright and hot, but not as hot as it will be later in the day. You sit on the concrete shelf, tell your name to a man carrying a clipboard and wearing a whistle on a string around his neck. He has skinny legs, a big gut, and very hairy forearms. His face reminds you of a coach at school. His body makes you wonder if he would float. "Everyone in the pool," he yells and blows his whistle. The guy beside you dives in head first. You walk to the steps and edge your way into the freezing water, stopping when you reach your waist. You wait a few seconds until your teeth start chattering and then you dip into the water to your shoulders, take a breath, and swim underwater. This is your favorite way to cool off in the heat.

When you emerge, the man with the whistle is addressing the guys in the class. There are twelve of you. He says his name is Mr. Williams. He gives a spiel on the importance of safety in the water and being serious about looking out for others and how swimming is a serious matter than can mean the difference between life and death. The guy beside you treads water. You stand in shallower water, on your tip toes, balancing yourself with your outstretched arms. You like to rock in the water as if you are dancing. While the instructor is talking, you sing pop songs in your head while you rock.

The first part of the class is the qualification. You have to swim and swim and swim. You do one lap, then have to do another, and then another. Mr. Williams yells to change from sidestroke to breaststroke. Your heart is beating in your ears. You swim and swim. Your chest is full of air one minute and gasping for more the next. Your lungs begin to hurt. Your arms grow heavy. When you finally finish the guy next to you is coughing up water. Mr. Williams blows his whistle and everyone gets out of the pool.

Next you have to retrieve a brick from the bottom of the pool. You are number seven. The first two boys are like seals. They easily retrieve the brick. The third guy doesn't like to open his eyes underwater. He has to dive several times to get the brick. Mr. Williams turns red in the face but seems to forget it when the fourth boy is a seal, too. When it is your turn you hold your breath and dive. You swim easily to the brick but find it heavier than you expected. The weight is a shock to you and it takes you a couple of seconds to get a good grip on it before you surface.

Mr. Williams taps you on the back when you get out of the pool and says, "Good job." You sit and catch your breath and watch the other boys dive and retrieve the brick. Number nine and number twelve struggle with the brick, too. Only number ten, a skinny boy with scabs on his knees, can't bring the brick to the surface.

Next you have to swim with the brick without using your hands. Mr. Williams begins the numbers backward, with boy twelve. Number ten keeps dropping the brick. You sit in the sun squinting, getting nervous. When it is your turn you jump into the pool holding the brick. When you surface Mr. Williams yells for you to swim with the brick and not dog-paddle in place. You hold the brick in front of you, as if it would float on its own. It doesn't. It can't. Your arms grow tired. Your legs become more tired. Your lungs hurt. You keep looking over your shoulder hoping Mr. Williams will blow his whistle when your time is up. When the whistle finally goes off you drop the brick. Mr. Williams yells at you, tells you to dive and pick it up and bring it back to the surface.

In the car after the class, your father asks you if you want to drive home. You shake your head no and turn on the radio.

o   o   o

The next day at the pool there are only ten boys in the class. You remember that number eight's name is Andy. Number five is Craig. Two is Steve, who was in your algebra class last year and never spoke to you because he is tall and on the basketball team and you are short and only in the marching band. You begin the class by swimming laps. Mr. Williams makes you tread water, surface dive for the brick, and swim laps with it before you get out of the pool. After class your mom picks you up and you drive the car home.

o   o   o

On Wednesday, you float. You spend minutes and minutes and minutes and minutes on your back with your stomach and eyes to the sky. The sun is very bright and you have to squint while you float. Water fills up your ears. Chlorine sinks into your skin.

After floating you practice tossing a rescue tube in the water. Water continues to stay in your ears. The chlorine makes you itch. While Mr. Williams is talking you keep shaking your head to dislodge the water and scratching your arm. Charlie, number six, keeps coughing so that you can't understand the instructions. Steve, the tall basketball player guy, picks dead skin from between his toes.

After class, your older brother picks you up. He does not let you drive home.

o   o   o

On Thursday, it is not so sunny. There are only nine boys in the class now. Number six, the guy who was always coughing up water, has decided to drop out. Mr. Williams gives a lecture about the importance of safety. As the sky grows cloudier, he says he will teach you how to resuscitate a victim. He makes you line up according to height. He breaks the class into pairs. Since you are now the shortest guy in the class, the odd one out, Mr. Williams tells the class that you have the honor of being his partner. And guinea pig. He makes you lie on your back on the cement. You feel silly, let out a giggle, then try to become serious. He kneels beside you, on his knees. He explains to the class how to open the victim's airway. (He tilts your head back so that your mouth opens.) He leans his face over you and tells the boys how to check a victim's breathing. (You feel a bit of sweat under your arms even though the air is cool.) He explains that if the breathing is not normal, pinch the nose and ventilate. (He presses his fingers against your nostrils and his lips cover your mouth. His mouth is moist and full of energy. The whistle around his neck thumps against your chest. You cannot understand anything else he is saying because all of this is a shock to your body.) When he pulls away from you, you hear someone snicker. Mr. Williams reminds the class that this is a serious matter.

When it comes time for the class to practice CPR, Mr. Williams lies down on the cement, tells you to practice with him. You lean over him. His face seems huge. The pores of his face are filled with stubbles of black hair. Hair grows up from the collar of his shirt. Behind you some boys giggle while they practice, others grunt and say to their partners, "Come on, just do it and get it over with."

Looking down at Mr. Williams, you don't think that you can stretch your mouth wide enough to cover his mouth. It is full of big teeth and a thick tongue. Stubbles of hair ring the border of his lips. You open your mouth wide, wider than a yawn, and press your mouth into his. You force two breaths of air into his mouth and realize, when you break away from him, that something of him remains with you. You cannot exactly place what it is. It is more than the taste of him. More than the moist, warm feeling of his mouth. Something, you think, has been left inside you.

When Mr. Williams tells the class to switch positions and continue practicing he stays on the ground. "Do it again," he says to you. "And don't be so nervous this time."

o   o   o

After CPR, Mr. Williams demonstrates how to handle a struggling victim. It is still too dark and gray and cold to swim. He continues to use you as the class guinea pig. "Don't sacrifice your life trying to save someone," he says. "If a victim lunges toward you, place an open hand against his chest."

Mr. Williams places the palm of his hand against your chest. His hand is moist and warm against your skin when he touches you. He turns you toward the class. "Lean backwards and submerge rapidly away from him. Keep your blocking arm extended."

Mr. Williams now takes his hand and presses it against your shoulder. His hand is so large you believe you can feel the weight of each of his fingers. He turns you away from the row of watching boys. He makes you clamp your tiny fingers around his thick, slippery, hairy wrist. "If a victim grabs your arm or wrist, quickly submerge the victim by reaching across with your free hand and pushing down on the victim's shoulder while kicking upward for better leverage," he says.

Mr. Williams presses against your shoulder so that you are forced to your knees. His strength is surprising, but his touch is still moist, warm. You look up at him as he says, "This leverage allows the rescuer to pull his hand free. You may also reach down with your free hand to grab your other hand, and jerk upward. Swim clear of the victim and reassess his condition."

Mr. Williams motions for you to stand up. He squats so that he is about your height. He takes both of your arms and places them around his shoulders. You can feel the power of his body. His eyes meet yours. "The front head hold escape technique allows you to escape from a victim who has thrown his arms around your head and neck," he says. "Take a quick breath and tuck your chin into a shoulder while shrugging your shoulders upwards. Then take a strong stroke and submerge instantly. This drags the victim below the water."

Mr. Williams shifts his squat so that he moves in closer to you. He moves his hands to rest below your elbows. His touch is surprisingly soft now. "Grasp the victim's elbows or the underside of the upper arms." You feel the energy building up in him. It seems to come from somewhere in his squat, somewhere in his legs. It moves up through his body until your hands are suddenly tossed up into the air. "You have to thrust the victim's arms upwards and away," he says while you are trying to reign in your thrashing arms. "Be sure to keep your chin tucked and shoulders shrugged to protect your throat."

The class ends with a demonstration of the wrist-tow and the cross-chest carry. Mr. Williams' hands surround you, warm you. His chest is against your back, your head is locked in his elbow. Then he is kneeling so that you can surround his chest with the hook of your arm. He looks up at you. You look down at him. You meet his stare. He meets yours. You feel his strength, the muscles in his arms, the strength in his legs, the dampness in the hair of his forearms—all within the clutch of the power of your elbow.

After class, the wind gives you a chill when you walk out to the car. Again, your brother does not let you drive home.

o   o   o

On Friday, you are back in the water. Mr. Williams is again your partner and he joins the class in the pool. He takes his shirt off and dives into the water without a splash. His body is huge and covered with wet black hair. You practice escapes and holds and tows with him for three hours. He keeps your energy focused on him.

o   o   o

Over the weekend, you tell your dad that you do not want to be a lifeguard because you want to work in the record store. He says no, that's no place for you to work. Your dad thinks Satan sends messages through certain kinds of music and books. Your mom does not dispute him. Your older brother, who smokes cigarettes sitting on the roof outside your bedroom window, tells you it's all a phony game so that adults can control the world.

Your mom lets you drive to the mall so that you don't spend all weekend inside reading a book. Your two younger sisters sing Bible camp songs in the backseat and make you nervous. You spend the whole time at the mall in the record store, forcing your littlest sister to find you and tell you when it's time to leave. Your mom is so annoyed at you for keeping her waiting that she does not let you drive home.

o   o   o

On Monday, Craig is not at class and Mr. Williams pairs you up with his partner, Steve. Practicing rescues and holds and tows with

Steve is not the same as it was with Mr. Williams. Steve has no coordination in the water. His grip is too tight. At one point you must knee him to prevent him from choking you. Since he is the largest boy in the class and you are the shortest, the rescues are awkward and you must fight off the urge to scream at him. By the end of the class you are so angry and upset that you decide you never want to come back to this pool again. You are glad to see your brother waiting for you in the parking lot. It means you don't even have to try to want to drive home.

o   o   o

On Tuesday, Craig is again out of class, though Mr. Williams does not say if he has dropped out for good or not. After twenty minutes of laps, you are once again paired with Steve. Each team of partners must demonstrate the rescue of a victim for the rest of the class. Since Steve is the tallest in the class, your demonstration is the last of the pairs. You sit in the sun while the four other teams thrash through the water. Andy and his partner use a float, which seems to sink the moment it is needed. When it is your team's turn, Steve decides that he will be the victim and you must rescue him with a cross-chest carry. Mr. Williams nods and Steve dives into the pool, swims to the deep end, and pretends to need help.

You dive into the pool, slice easily through water. You swim toward Steve. Steve grabs you by your left wrist when you are close to him. He is strong enough to push you underwater before you have a chance to react. You are smart enough to remember how to break the grip underwater, but when you surface Steve is behind you and grasping his long thin arms around your neck. You go back underwater to release his grip, like you have practiced, but his legs are so long and awkward you misjudge his thrashing. He kicks you first in the arm. Then in the stomach.

The air goes out of you while you are underwater. You feel water rushing into your mouth. At first, everything goes blurry. Then, everything goes black. When you blink your eyes open, you are lying on the tiles at the edge of the pool. Mr. Williams is leaning over you. His face is close to yours. You can taste him inside of you. He has saved you from Steve. He has saved you from drowning.

After class, you wait in the car while Mr. Williams talks with your father. You see the disappointment register on your dad's face as he walks to the car. He asks you if you want to drive home. You shake your head no. You don't want to talk to him. He doesn't understand what happened. He doesn't understand that Steve kicked the wind out of you. You feel like crying. You don't want to be a lifeguard but you don't want to be a failure, either. About a block from home, your dad says that Mr. Williams wants you to take the class again next year. "You just need to be stronger and older," your dad says. "It'll help you keep up with the bigger boys."

You decide your older brother is actually right about something. The world is a conspiracy of adults. And bigger boys.

o   o   o

Ten years later you are two inches taller and thirty-three pounds heavier than you were the summer you drowned and were saved by Mr. Williams. You remember the swimming class while you are at the gym. The memory doesn't happen right away. It floats to the surface when a guy steps on a treadmill next to the one you are using. You see his face in the mirror in front of you. It is not the same face, but it is similar enough to dislodge the whole set of memories of what happened the summer you were fifteen. It is not the same body either, but the stocky, hairy build is enough to make you remember Mr. Williams.

You walk on the treadmill until it is comfortable enough to jog. You run at a slow pace, keeping your steps even. You glance in the mirror. Yes, the face is similar. Too similar. It is the same nose, the same wide stubble of blue-black hairs. The same jaw. Your throat tightens. For the next twenty-two minutes you remember everything you can of Mr. Williams and then you want to forget him.

After the treadmill, you move to the other exercise equipment. You are ready to repack the memories now that you have examined them. You move from the leg machine to the back machine to the bicep machine. You don't look back at the guy on the treadmill. Your life moves forward. Your workout continues. You lie on the mat and do sit-ups. When you finish and walk across the room to the free weights, you notice he is no longer on the treadmill. A quick glance through the room shows you that he is no longer on this floor. You relax and continue exercising. By the time you make it to the locker room you have forgotten him. The memories have been repacked.

You change into your swimsuit and take a quick shower. You walk out of the changing room into the small corridor that leads to the Jacuzzi. This part of the gym is coed, used by both male and female members. It is a large, glass-enclosed space in the area between the entrances to the men and women's locker rooms. Since there is so much walking back and forth in front of the glass wall, most members don't use the wet sauna because it is like sitting inside a television set. Everyone looks to see what you are doing. You hate this part of the gym, too, though you love sitting in the hot tub for a few minutes before you change back into your everyday clothes and walk across town to your apartment.

Today, the water is hotter than usual but you adjust to it easily. You are the only person in the Jacuzzi. You lie back with your head against the ledge of tiles, going through a list of things you want to do before going to work tomorrow morning, the faint smell of chlorine haunting your memory. You close your eyes to concentrate and relax, even though the gym is emptier than usual today because it is a summer weekend. Most of the members are out of town or out at a private beach somewhere. (Your soon-to-expire membership was a generous gift from a boyfriend who has already expired beyond his usefulness. You could never afford this kind of place on the kind of money you make as a proofreader at a law firm and the larger amount you owe in student loans, so you journey across town as often as you can to use this gym.)

When you open your eyes, only a few seconds later, you are surprised to see him entering the hot tub. It is like you have entered a dream. Or a dreamworld. You cannot believe this is happening but you cannot decide if it is pleasure or torture.

He takes the steps slowly into the water. His body is covered with dark hair that becomes darker when wet. He is wearing a small black swimsuit. He stretches his arms out on top of the water, dips his body in and out. He does not look at you as he settles into the water beside you. At this point you have decided it is torture. You think about leaving but you are too embarrassed to step out of the Jacuzzi. You are already aroused. You would have to reveal all that you have. You cannot leave the Jacuzzi until you can find a way to hide your interest in him.

You try not to stare at him. You look at the empty hallway, the empty walkway, the streaks of humidity on the glass wall. He stretches out his legs in front of him and flutter kicks. His leg grazes against yours. He pretends not to notice it has happened. You pretend it has not happened, either.

He shifts in closer to you. You shift in closer to him. He changes position, dips his body up and down, his hands now underwater. His touch grazes you. He pretends it has not happened. His face is a warm, stubbly stare. He is a torture-machine and you will not let him know it. You pretend he has not touched you either. Your heart is beating in your ears.

He shifts closer to you. Underwater, his hand presses against your swimsuit. You glance over his shoulder. You look again at the empty hallway, the empty walkway. Your face does not reveal your pleasure though your body reveals every inch of it. You are flushed with blood. When you move your hand to his swimsuit, you feel he is erect, too. He is ready for you. He is a torture-machine of pleasure, you decide. His face remains motionless as you shift your hand inside his swimsuit. When he touches you, he easily finds what he wants.

The encounter continues without conversation or interruption. Your facial expression does not change to accommodate his stroking hand. His black-stubbly jaw does not shift to recognize yours. All of this continues out of sight, underwater. He has easily aroused you because he is so familiar. At one moment you close your eyes and imagine he is Mr. Williams. Seconds later this is all over. The water has revealed nothing that has happened. The man has been satisfied and he is leaving the wet sauna. You watch his black swimsuit and furry black legs disappear into the locker room. After all these years, this fantasy is over as quickly as you can come.

When you are alone again in the water, you shake your head, trying to dislodge water that has somehow become trapped in your left ear. Your father told you the day that Mr. Williams saved your life that your instructor was willing to make an exception and keep you in the class if you wanted to remain, though he didn't think that you would pass the final examinations and get your lifesaving certificate. Your father had decided it was not the right path for you, that one close encounter with death was enough to chance in a summer.

"He's a fast learner," Mr. Williams had said to your dad. "A few more years and he'll be a strong swimmer, too."

You realize it has taken ten years to understand how smart you were that summer. You never forgot the taste of that something Mr. Williams left in your mouth when his lips pressed his breath into yours. It was not something that you could easily explain at age fifteen. But it was also something you knew you could not let drown.

What You Pay

Your first mistake was to say yes. Of course you wanted to go to Atlantic City. Of course you weren't doing anything else today.

Your second mistake was to choose the row behind them. You could see them smooching through the crack. Keith and Peter. Kiss, kiss, kiss. You should have sat in front of them, so you wouldn't be distracted from the library book you brought—a book of stories by F. Scott Fitzgerald. You look out the window, at the view of the New Jersey turnpike. The road is gray. The sky is gray. The cars are colorless blurs. Whatever were you thinking when you said yes to a trip to Atlantic City in the wintertime?

For months Keith has been going on about Atlantic City, how it would be fun to get a group together for a trip, play the casinos, walk on the boardwalk, sit on the beach. Keith is a new friend. You meet frequently for off-Broadway plays, movie screenings, concerts at Lincoln Center. Keith has a knack for getting free tickets. He calls you at the last minute to go with him. How does he know that you never have any other plans?

You look at your watch, shake your wrist. The watch needs a battery but you don't have the money to replace it. If you shake the watch a couple of times a day the battery keeps working. This is what it is like to be twenty-five years old and poorer than a Bowery bum. You have twelve dollars and fourteen cents in a checking account. You are one month behind on the rent and owe thousands of dollars in student loans. You have fifteen dollars in your wallet and thirty-five cents in your pocket. What could you possibly win in Atlantic City?

Now you hear them. They are giggling and whispering. You see Peter's eye through the crack looking at you. You look down at your book. Think about the Jazz Age. Flappers, Gatsby, Zelda. You open the book, read a few words, worry some more about money. At least the bus fare is free. At least Keith found a casino that pays customers to visit.

You read a story about a rich boy. He has a chauffeur that drives him to the Ritz and the kind of servants "you can't get anymore." The kind of life you do not have, have not had, will not have. His misfortunes with love do not resonate with you. Fitzgerald is right. The very rich are very different. Especially from you.

You are about to start another story when the bus leaves the highway. A gray town comes into view, blocks and blocks of shabby life. The bus makes a sharp left turn, enters a covered parking lot next to a tall, modern building. Keith sticks his head over the back of his seat, says in a sing-songy voice. "We're here. Get your money ready."

The bus driver hands you a roll of quarters when you step off the bus. This casino even pays customers to gamble. At least you are ten dollars ahead. At least you can say you earned ten bucks today by riding a bus. You follow Keith and Peter through a corridor, wait for an elevator. Two minutes and three floors later you are inside a casino.

You follow Keith to a slot machine, watch him unwrap his quarters, spill them into a plastic cup. The room is noisy. Ching-ching-ching, coins dropping into metal trays. Levers are pulled, gears click into place, wheels spin, spin, spin. Stop with a cluck-cluck-cluck.

Keith loses his ten dollars quickly. Peter says he is going to play blackjack. Peter is noisy, garish, reminds you of a slot machine. Keith pulls out a ten dollar bill from his wallet and goes to get change. You are faced with the room—the red carpet, the circling lights, the people hypnotized like zombies.

You tell Keith you want to walk around. You look at your watch and shake it. You tell him you will meet him back at the bus. He does not even protest. He nods his head. Up and down. He puts three more quarters into a slot machine and pulls the lever. He is a zombie.

Outside it is cold. The sky still gray. There is a possibility of snow. The thought makes you smile. You walk to the edge of the boardwalk. Snow, sand, sea, a combination you've never seen.

You walk to a store with a big glass window, bright lights inside. You look through the window at the jars of candy. Your eyes feel heavy. You want to take a nap but you go inside the store, buy a small bag of salt water taffy that costs two dollars.

You walk and chew. Chew and walk. The taffy swells in your stomach. The chewing keeps you warm, the sugar coats your teeth. You feel the weight of the roll of quarters in your pants pocket. You are still eight dollars ahead. You walk inside another casino. Look at the zombies, listen to the noise. You can smell cigarette smoke trapped in the red rug, so you leave.

You walk some more outside. Look at the water, the store windows, go briefly inside a T-shirt shop. It is too cold to sit on the boardwalk and read. You are too poor to gamble. You walk back to the first casino, find the elevator to the parking deck. You sit in a hall and read till your eyes are heavy, then lean your head against the wall. Your skull vibrates. You swear you can hear the casino three floors down. The ching-ching-ching, cluck-cluck-cluck. You take a deep breath and close your eyes. You wake up about an hour later when someone comes through the elevator doors.

You look at your watch. Shake your wrist. There is another hour till the bus comes. You read some more, nap a few more minutes, then eat a piece of taffy.

You get to the bus early. The parking lot is cold. You eat some more taffy, think about looking for some water but then decide to wait.

You wait. You wait and wait. Soon everyone is aboard the bus except for you, Keith, and Peter.

The bus driver says he will be leaving in three minutes. You shake your wrist, look at your watch. Now there is a dilemma.

Leave them behind? Go back to the city without them? What if something has happened—why hasn't one of them shown up?

You wave good-bye to the bus driver. You wait inside the hall where it is not so cold. You are too worried to eat the last piece of taffy. You feel the roll of quarters in your pocket. You try to read your book but cannot concentrate. You think about how much it will cost to catch a different bus back to New York.

Keith shows up twenty minutes late. Peter is not with him. Peter is down two hundred dollars and is not ready to go back. Keith says there is another bus in three hours, and another one three hours after that. He does not share your worry: There is always another bus back to the city. You tell Keith you are taking the next bus back. He says, "Let's go get something to eat. I've got a headache."

You take the stairs down to the ground floor. You walk away from the boardwalk, into the shabby part of town. It is dark and colder. Keith goes inside a liquor store. He asks for a bottle of bourbon, turns and says, "You got any money? I didn't win anything."

You pull the roll of quarters out of your pocket. He looks at you, says, "You didn't play them?"

You shake your head. He unwraps some quarters, hands them to the cashier—a woman with dyed blond hair and raccoon-like eyes. Keith folds the top of the roll down against the unspent quarters, hands it back to you.

Outside, Keith opens the bottle. Takes a sip, says, "Ummmm." He passes the bottle to you. You take a sip. The liquor burns your stomach, gets the digesting taffy all bubbly, makes you feel bloated. You follow Keith down the street and into a diner.

Keith orders a fish sandwich and fries. You order soup. You make light conversation. Keith says his head is splitting, maybe the food will make him feel better.

You eat in silence. Keith is not talking anymore. When the bill comes, you look at it on the table, wait to see if Keith reaches for the bill or his wallet. You begin to sweat, thinking you ought to pick up the tab. Keith took you to a screening last week. And a play in the Village. And a gallery opening in Soho.

You pay the bill, leave a tip from the roll of quarters. Outside the diner, there is a group of guys smoking. They watch you walk by. You worry they will rob you. What will they do when they find you have nothing? Keith stops a few feet from the tallest of the guys, bends over to the curb, throws up.

The guys stop smoking, stub out their cigarettes, walk away disgusted. You ask Keith if he is okay. He says his head is splitting and he feels like he is going to faint. "I'm not gonna make it," he says. "Let's go get a room."

You think he is kidding. You say: "You don't want to wait for the bus?"

"I wanna lie down now," he says. The tone of his voice is like someone spoiled, like a character in a Fitzgerald story.

Keith follows you to casino. It is a slow and painful walk. You ask him if he needs a doctor, if he wants to go to the emergency room instead of getting a room. He says no, he only wants to lie down. He wants to get a room and lie down on a bed.

Inside the casino, you ask a clerk about a room in the hotel. He quotes some prices and you pick the lowest. You hand him your last credit card, the only one which has not been canceled. You expect it to be revoked any day. Your payment is late. You owe money from the gifts you sent your family for Christmas, the family that is in another state and that never calls but always expects gifts.

The clerk does not check on the status of the credit card. You sign a registration form. The clerk hands you keys to the room. You ask Keith about Peter's whereabouts. Keith sits in a chair beside a slot machine and waits while you find Peter at a blackjack table and give him the extra room key.

Inside the room, Keith crashes on one of the beds. He closes his eyes and never wakes up, even when you are surfing channels on the TV. You cannot relax. You expect a knock at the door at any moment. Someone saying to vacate the room because you cannot pay. Keith is no help because he looks like he is dead. You check his breathing and see that he is still alive, his chest going up and down. Up and down.

You walk to the window, look at a construction site, an air-conditioning unit on a roof, a parking lot. There is no snow. You cannot see the sea. Just a gray night.

You pull your book out of your bag. Place it on the night table. You pour a glass of bourbon. Decide to watch TV instead of read, an old black-and-white movie with a silly, serious soundtrack. Keith rotates, changes position, throws a fist into a pillow.

"Is this too loud?"

He does not respond. Soon he starts snoring. He feels miserable but he is not in misery because someone like you is watching out for him. You watch the end of the movie. You surf channels some more, close your eyes, fall asleep with the TV on.

You wake when Peter bumps into the chair. "Hey," you say.

"Hey," he answers back.

Keith is still snoring. Peter unbuttons his shirt.

"Did you win?"

"Huh?"

"Did you win?"

"Only down four hundred," he says. "Maybe I'll try again later."

Four hundred, you think. You could become solvent with four hundred. You roll over, clutch the pillow, say, "You can turn off the TV."

"Uh huh," he answers.

You close your eyes, fall into sleep. It is dark when you wake sometime later. Someone is in bed beside you. At first you think it is a dream. Then you realize it isn't. You feel an arm around your waist, breath against your neck. You move into the embrace, not away from it. This surprises you. How you react.

"Hey," you hear.

"Hey," you say back.

"It was cold over there," he says. He draws you into a kiss. He moves his tongue into your mouth. You taste the alcohol of him. He has had some of the bourbon. He runs his hand down your thigh, back up to your groin. He feels your dick. It is hard. He strokes it a moment, cups your balls, kneads them.

You think of no one but yourself. You are barely breathing. He is breathing heavily. Or is that Keith, still snoring? He rolls on top of you. You feel the weight of him. He rubs his dick against your body. You feel the heat, the friction of him. He pulls the covers off. You feel the chill of the room, the warmth of him on top of you, his tongue in your mouth.

He shifts so that you roll on your side. He moves so that your face is between his legs. You do not resist any part of him. At the moment of climax, he rolls toward you, his come hits your shoulder.

You remain like that for a few minutes, lost in the leg and thigh and hair and groin of him. He rolls over and wipes himself dry with the bedsheet. The cold hits your sweat like ice water when he breaks away. The bed bounces as it releases his weight when he stands.

You hear his feet on the carpet, the sheet being lifted away from the other bed. You reach for the pillow, clutch it, notice that Keith has stopped snoring. You close your eyes but cannot fall asleep. What price will you have to pay for this?

You feel like you have lost a fortune.

o   o   o

The next morning Peter orders room service. He has a cheese and onion omelet, hash browns, bacon, and a screwdriver. Keith has wheat toast. You order coffee and scrambled eggs. The attendant arrives while Peter is in the shower. Keith says he still feels weak, does not move from the bed. You answer the door and sign the bill to the room.

After breakfast you shower. When you come out of the bathroom, Peter and Keith are gone. Keith has left a note. "We're down in the casino."

You take the unwrapped bar of soap and the unused tiny bottles of conditioner and moisturizing lotion and put them in your bag. At the counter downstairs, you check the bill. Can you go to jail for doing this? You think about all the things you could have bought with this money. You think about the benefits of jail—no rent, three free meals, plenty of sex with other guys.

You find Keith in the casino before you leave. You tell him you are taking the next bus back. He is putting more quarters in a slot machine. You feel for the remainder of the roll of quarters in your pocket but it is gone. Keith nods at the slot machine and puts another set of quarters in. He is in zombie land. He says he got an advance off of his credit card. He says, "It was real easy. I should have done this yesterday."

On the bus trip back you look in your bag for your book. It is gone. It is upsetting to discover this. You feel distraught, defeated. How much does it costs to replace a library book? A library book about rich Jazz Age flappers. Why did you even want to read about the rich? You wonder if this book was a first edition, if it is irreplaceable, if writing about rich people means it will cost more.

You watch the gray highway change into another gray highway. You think about what would happen if you started dating Peter. What would Keith do if you told him you slept with his new boyfriend? How much would a confession like this cost you?

You total up the price of a dinner, a movie, and an off-Broadway theater ticket and decide it's not worth the effort. You have no interest in dating Peter. And you'd rather not lose Keith as a friend.

But you are not home free. You are not exempt. You know you will pay a price for your indiscretion. You know the bill will arrive someday soon.

What Counts Most

Your discomfort mounts. It is too cold in the shade and too bright in the sun. On the street corner where you are waiting there is no in-between spot. You must either shiver or squint. You decide you look better shivering than squinting so you step into the shade and wait. While you are shivering in a neighborhood where you never like to be in the first place you are tormented by feeling overweight even though you have lost three pounds since last week. You try to look relaxed but feel your forehead tense into anxious ridges. You are waiting for a man who is impossibly handsome, possibly the most handsome man you have ever met in the city, even though you know he lives somewhere outside of it in a place that you have never been to. You are waiting to spend a weekend with this handsome man. His handsomeness makes you insecure about your own looks. Very insecure. You feel like you've gained weight just waiting for him to show up, even though you are certain your chattering teeth are burning up a few calories.

You are waiting on his route to the tunnel. Everyone who passes you on the sidewalk is able to regulate his body temperature except for you. A large, muscular man in a sleeveless T-shirt goes by eating an ice cream bar. A toothless homeless woman wrapped in a blanket pushes a shopping cart filled with empty plastic bottles. The smell of beer or urine or both surrounds you and the pile of garbage you are standing beside. A fly torments you while you shiver in the morning air. Minutes pass. You look out into the street, thinking you will recognize his car even though you have never seen it before. What possessed you to agree to spend the weekend with this guy? His handsomeness? Or just being around him, breathing in the possibility of such beauty?

You imagine him arriving to find you shivering, parking his car, warming you up by rubbing his hands along your shoulders, and drawing you into a deep, silky kiss. Then somewhere from behind his back he presents you with flowers. Or chocolates. Or chocolate flowers that are calorie-free, saying he has thought about nothing except you since the last time you were together.

A passing truck sends a gust of hot dust into your eyes. You step further back into the cold shade. Nothing like that will happen of course. This is not a romantic outing. You don't expect him to arrive with gifts. He may not even kiss you. The last time you saw him you lay side by side in a hotel bed without even touching. He would not kiss you. He would not let you kiss him. He would not touch your body. He would not let you touch his.

"I can't risk it," he said, and he stroked his big beautiful cock and you stroked your smaller, more imperfect one. His handsomeness made your orgasm easy even though he made you feel like a bag of festering germs. So why are you even bothering to see him again? When a car stops beside you your body surges with blood. You are again reminded that he is the most handsome man you have ever met in this city, even though he is not a resident of it. Of course you are going to see him again. Of course you will wait in the middle of nowhere for him to pick you up to take you out of the city to somewhere in the country for the weekend. Of course you won't do whatever he doesn't want you to do because, after all, being around someone so beautiful is nothing to take seriously.

o   o   o

In the car you feel your anxiety mounting. He is just as good-looking as he was the last time you saw him, even though you were dizzy from the aftermath of two martinis when you started talking with him. He might even be better looking now because your vision is not as blurry as it was when you were drinking. Yes, you decide, he is better looking than the last time you saw him. This makes you feel more inadequate. He is wearing a blue cotton button-down shirt that highlights his eyes. You wonder if he can tell by the T-shirt that you are wearing that your stomach is not flat enough to have ridges of muscle showing. Of course he can tell, you remind yourself, he's seen you without the T-shirt. He knows exactly how much weight you have and where you have it, except for the three missing pounds since last week. You wonder if he can tell you have lost three pounds.

"You got your hair cut," he says.

Yes, you think, he can tell you lost three pounds. Three pounds of hair is missing from your head since last week, since the cheap barber you go to went a little too crazy when you were crazy enough to ask him for a quick trim because you wanted to look perfect for the perfect man this weekend.

You don't ask him if he likes your haircut. You will not set yourself up for disappointment, even though you are desperate to receive a compliment from him because it would be a compliment from a truly handsome man. "It's shorter," you say.

"It makes you look younger," he says.

You are not certain if this is a compliment or not, but the sound of his voice makes you nod and smile. You watch him drive around a circular ramp and merge into the traffic disappearing into the tunnel. You met this man at a bar last week. His name is Jack and he is forty-six years old. It is no joke to you that the digits of his age add up to the number ten. He is a perfect man. An all-around ten. At least in the looks department. He could be a movie star. Or a politician. You are certain he is popular with everyone who knows him for what he is: a very handsome man.

But this is also a handsome man with a few too many flaws, though you do not let them bother you and you do not subtract any digits from the total count of his overall appearance. One flaw is a wife named Colleen. In a less handsome man this would knock him down a digit or two. Two other flaws are a daughter named Annie and a son named Wes. He could lose a few points for these two other things, as well, though this married man named Jack with two kids does not lose even a fraction of a point for having them. Another flaw is that his family does not know he is not where he has told them he will be and he is with someone they would not approve of if they did know where he was. This gorgeous, closeted married man named Jack does not lose any digits for this, either, though if any other guy had lied to you or about you and you had discovered the lie and the secret, his digits would be turned into a negative number.

When the car emerges from the tunnel the sunlight makes you squint. You realize you forgot to bring your sunglasses. Why didn't you remember to bring your sunglasses? This perfect man will now be reduced to watching you squint the entire day. This thought makes you break into a sweat. You are twenty-nine years old and worried about the way you look when you are squinting and how flat your stomach appears when you are sitting in the bucket seat of a car. Your stomach is not that imperfect, you remind yourself, even though you can do nothing to prevent the squinting. Your stomach might not be flat enough to see your ab muscles through the skin but you would also not lose any points for the way it looks, either. Your waist is the same size it was when you were in college. Your waist size is the same two digits as your age.

"I'm starving," Jack says. "You don't mind if I stop somewhere to get something to eat, do you?"

Of course you don't mind, noting he did not ask if you were hungry, too, but accepting because of the way he looks it is acceptable for him to be self-involved and not thinking of your hunger. Yes, you think, swirling in the irony of your own self-involved fantasy: He is hungry and does not lose any points for being self-involved because he is hungry for someone just like you.

o o o

He could lose a few points for the way he chews, too, because it forces you to look at the food in his mouth and not at his beautiful, gorgeous, handsome face. While he talks about his car with his mouth full of food, you look at the couple at the next table eating hamburgers and sharing a plate of French fries even though it is barely noon. They are incredibly overweight. Their buttons pull and their zippers strain. They are as extremely overweight as Jack is extremely handsome. But they chew their food with their mouths closed.

You try not to slip into a bad mood because you are looking at an overweight couple eat instead of the handsome man in front of you chew with his mouth open. You eat your frozen yogurt. The cold surge in your mouth creates an instant headache. You squint and grimace and groan. The bad mood has arrived. It is in full force inside your skull. You hope it does not destroy the weekend. You will try to keep it to yourself. You will try not to take your bad mood out on an extremely handsome self-involved closeted married man.

"What are you staring at?" he says, as if he is talking to a child. He has noticed you are no longer looking at him.

"I'm not," you answer. "I must have just been lost in thought."

"What were you thinking about?" he asks. He grins like he is running for election.

"Nothing," you answer. "I was thinking about nothing because this yogurt was giving me a headache."

He gives you another kind of grin, a shift of the lips, this one strained at the corners.

You realize that you are now on the path of ruining his weekend. You try to salvage the conversation by changing the direction back to him. "Where did you get that shirt?" you ask. "It goes good with your eyes."

The smile widens again; the first kind, the natural kind, is back. "I have them made for me," he says. "A tailor from Hong Kong does them. He comes to the city once a year and I order a new set of them."

"How many do you have?"

"A lot," he answers. "I change colors every year. I have a lot of white, some striped, even a pink one, though I don't wear that one much."

"Why not?"

"It feels obvious," he says.

Of course it does, you think. An extremely handsome man in a pink shirt. Even a set of kids will not deflect that.

"A few years ago I even had monograms put on the cuffs," he says.

"The pink one?"

"Of course not," he answers. "It was blue and white striped. You could barely detect the initials in the pattern. It was very subtle, like it wasn't even there unless you were expecting to find it."

That certainly makes sense, you think, hiding something where no one will notice it.

o   o   o

You squint for another hour. And then for another hour. The city gives way to suburbs which change to farm land. The yogurt gives you gas, which makes you silently grimace and squirm and squint some more. The land changes into hills. The highway crosses a river and goes around a mountain. The conversation in the car shifts from his tailored business suits to the house he designed back to his custom-built car (which is incredibly expensive and uncomfortable). For the last hour the radio has been on. Top 40 has now been replaced with country music.

When he parks at the lodge, you follow him up a set of wooden stairs, your head bowed to the ground to avoid the sun. In the lobby he continues to walk ahead of you, and you clasp your hands behind your back to complete the feeling that you are merely a geisha following three steps behind a great man.

At the counter you watch a sleepy-eyed clerk, not much older than you, drop his jaw when Jack's attractiveness begins to register with him. His expression becomes bug-eyed when Jack asks about a reservation. Jack gives the man two names you have never heard before—certainly not yours and definitely not his own. When Jack asked you to spend the weekend with him, he said a friend owed him a favor and could get a room in an out-of-the-way country lodge. He didn't tell you any other details about the friend, which makes you believe that he didn't tell the friend any details about you, either.

You notice that there is no credit card exchanged when the clerk blushes and looks for keys. No cash is exchanged between them, either. This has all been arranged days before, though unbeknownst to the clerk, Jack's handsomeness is completely unexpected. While you are waiting you realize you have not told anyone where you are going for the weekend or that you were spending it with an extremely attractive closeted married man. You wonder if that was wise. You wonder if you should have told someone where you were going and why you were doing it. Maybe someone could have talked you out of it.

As you follow Jack out of the lobby he says, "I hope you don't mind that we got two rooms. I'm a light sleeper."

You are so stunned that you cannot respond. You feel as if someone—a giant puppeteer above you—is nodding your head for you. You follow Jack down a corridor, around a corner, and into another hallway.

"You can have the room at the end of the hall," he says. "I'll take this one."

He hands you a key and unlocks the door where he has stopped. "I'm going to take a quick nap," he says. "All that sun and driving has made me a little edgy."

No sense in both of us being in a bad mood, you think, as you continue down the hall to your room.

o o o

Your room does not surprise you. It is small and has a view of a parking lot. You try to decide if you are more disappointed in the size of the room, the lack of an interesting view, or the fact that you are alone, spending a weekend with a too handsome, too closeted, married man who has decided he wants to sleep in separate rooms. You grow angry when you realize that this has all been planned in advance. He has always planned that you would be in separate rooms. All you can think about is how to get out of this. Your weekend is destroyed. You are humiliated. You are not even young and attractive enough to share a room with. You open your wallet and try to calculate if you have enough money to call a cab to drive you back into the city. No such luck. You barely have enough for food.

Your headache grows wider. It moves from a point above your left eye to a larger point between both of your eyes to an even larger point somewhere near your hairline. You are in agony. Your head is hurting so much now you have to close your eyes.

In the bathroom while you are taking an aspirin you smell something strange. You breathe in the foul odor, breathe out, and breathe it in again, thinking it will not be there this time. No such luck. The stench is still there. You look at the glass you just drank from. It looks clean. You smell the water. Nothing. It smells okay. You stick your nose closer to the tub, then the sink, then the toilet. You decide your bathroom must be sitting on top of a septic tank. Your headache shifts to the other eye. You wobble into the room and lie down on the narrow single bed. Maybe a nap will make everything go away. Or maybe a nap will make things seem better.

o   o   o

The phone startles you. The room is dark even though the curtains are open. Hours have passed. Or at least it seems as if hours have passed. You fumble around the room for the light switch, find the knob for the lamp, and flick it on. The phone is so loud you think it might jump off the table if you do not answer it.

"I must have been really tired," Jack says when you answer the phone. "Let's get something to eat."

"Okay," you answer and hang up the phone. Your headache is gone, you realize, or at least it is temporarily hiding from you. You put on your shoes and ignore the smell from the bathroom. You meet Jack at the door to his room.

"The restaurant downstairs is supposed to be good," he says and locks the door behind him.

He leads the way. You follow three steps behind him with your arms behind your back. The nap has freshened your wit. Or deepened it. You have decided that if he can humiliate you with separate rooms you can at least mock his attractiveness by pretending to be his geisha.

In the dining room everyone stares at Jack. The bartender, the waitress, the busboy, the couple at the next table and the table after that one. You find great comfort in knowing that if something were to happen to you, if you were to be murdered in your sleep in the middle of this nowhere lodge, everyone would remember that he was here this weekend at this particular lodge, though you doubt that they would remember you, the way you looked, or the person you were. "Was he the scowling one?" the bartender might ask. "No, he was the one in the T-shirt with the not-so-flat stomach," the waitress would say. The busboy would probably pinpoint you as the dreamy-eyed guy who looked like he had a headache coming on. The couple at the table next to you would say, "Oh yes, he was the geisha, wasn't he? What was that all about anyway?"

There is a candle at the center of your table. A flower in a vase is near the left ledge, closest to the window. The mountain rises outside. It is very romantic but you will not succumb to this setup any further. You now pretend that Jack is not so good-looking. You pretend he is just a normal, average, ordinary gorgeous-looking guy in a beautiful hand-tailored blue shirt with a wife and two kids who know nothing about you. It does not surprise you that the conversation during dinner revolves around him. There is some discussion about his clothes. He talks briefly about how much money he makes at his job.

After dinner Jack suggests you go back upstairs for the night since he has no clue of how to find town or if there is even a town nearby. You think this is a smart idea because you do not wish to be any more lost with him than you already are. Following him through the corridor, around the corner, and through the other hallway you realize that you did not bring a book to read to fill up the upcoming empty hours. The reception on the TV is probably lousy in your stinky room. What are you going to do until you are ready to go back to sleep?

You don't even stop at his door when he pulls his key out to unlock his room. You continue down the hall feeling defeated. After a few steps you sense that something is amiss. You hear him, over your shoulder, say, in a strange and childish voice, "Don't you want to visit for a while?"

You turn and give him a surprised look. "Sure," you answer and follow him inside his room.

His room surprises you. No, it flabbergasts you. It is the size of a suite. A lavish suite. There is a couch and a fireplace. On the floor is a furry dead animal that has a nose and a mouth with a wide set of teeth.

"Damn," he says, standing in front of a huge, wooden-framed mirror. "I got stains all over my shirt."

"I'm sure they'll wash out," you say. You do not mention that he got them from chewing with his mouth open.

"Nope," he answers. "It's oil. From the salad, I guess. Or the sauce. The shirt is ruined. I'll just have to toss it out now."

"You're throwing the shirt away?"

"It'll never look the same," he says. "Those stains won't come out. Colleen tries and tries and she just can't get rid of them."

"But it's such a beautiful shirt," you say. "You just can't throw it out."

"You want it?" he asks.

He begins to unbutton the shirt. Blood surges through your body. Your mouth drops open. You can barely breathe. You cannot decide if you are more amazed that he is willing to give you the shirt off his back or that he is standing there undressing before you.

When the shirt is off he tosses it to you. Your hands lift to catch it, as if the puppeteer is back, deciding what motions he will allow you to make. Your eyes follow Jack as he moves shirtless through the room. He crosses to his suitcase, unlocks it, then sits on a stool and begins to untie his shoes.

"I've got a surprise for you," he says.

You sit on the arm of the couch, or, rather, the puppeteer makes you fold your legs so that the arm of the couch can support your weight that is three pounds less than it was a few days ago.

"A surprise?" you ask. You think someone is also now throwing his voice into your body. The puppeteer is also speaking. You have no idea who you are anymore.

Jack unzips his pants and steps out of them, folding the legs of the pants carefully over the edge of a chair. He is now down to a set of boxers and a pair of socks. He leans against the chair and removes the socks.

"What kind of surprise?" you ask.

Jack opens the suitcase and waves you over to it. "I want you to help me," he says.

You walk across the room, barely missing stepping inside the mouth of the furry dead animal on the floor. You look into the open suitcase and see three, no, four dildos of varying sizes. There is a long, skinny one. A short stubby one with a handle, that looks more like a short plug. There is one about the size and shape of Jack's dick, as you recall the size and shape of it from the last time you were together. And another one that is much bigger. Much, much bigger than any normal or, as it goes, large dick should be.

"I've never done anything like this before," he says. "I want you to help me get used to it."

"Where did you get these?" you ask him.

"In the city," he says. "Not far from the place where I met you."

o   o   o

The suitcase yields more surprises: a bottle of wine, a corkscrew, plastic gloves, and a bottle of lubricant. Jack opens the wine, pours himself a glass in a cup he finds in the bathroom, and stretches towels on top of the bed so the sheets will not be ruined. "Have a glass," he says to you. "You should be relaxed too."

You wonder if he can tell that you are tense, or if he can tell that one specific part of your body is very, very tense and the rest of you is sweating. While he arranges the dildos on the bed you pour yourself a glass of wine and realize that you are part of a plan that a gorgeous, closeted, married man has been hatching probably long before he ever met you. "Take your shoes off and stay a while," he says, and adds a little laugh. His grin is from ear to ear. "Get comfortable," he says and laughs again.

You take off your shoes and then your pants. You keep your socks and T-shirt and underwear on, the T-shirt hiding the growing tense part of your body that is growing more and more tense as you watch Jack move around the room wearing only a pair of boxers.

The boxers come off next. He lies on the bed on top of the towels. He is flat on his back. His dick is not entirely hard but not entirely soft, either. You wish you had a camera so you could capture the perfect look of the perfect man stretched out in a perfect pose, but you know a camera is not necessary. This is a sight you will not soon forget. He tells you to put on the plastic gloves. He says he can't take any chances. He doesn't mention the wife and kids though you know he is thinking of them because he believes that you are a bag of festering germs ready to attack him.

You snap the gloves on.

You lather your fingers up with lubricant and then lubricate his asshole. He looks down at you at the end of the bed, as if you were a doctor examining his body. You, of course, *are* examining his body. Every inch and curve and glorious muscle of it. You watch him breathe. You tell him to breathe. You tell him to relax. You watch him relax. Your finger goes in and out of his rectum. When he is comfortable, you put another finger inside him. When he is ready, you lubricate the long, thin dildo.

While you push the dildo in and out he fondles his dick and balls. He grows harder. He closes his eyes. You imagine that he has decided that you are no longer here. Someone else is doing this to him—*his* fantasy man. His perfect man is penetrating him, giving him the pleasure he so desperately desires. He strokes and kneads while you push the dildo in and out. Your mind wanders from one part of his body to the next. You fight off your own urges to fondle yourself, stroke yourself, substitute yourself for the dildo that is in your hand pumping in and out of his ass.

After a while, he allows you to use the larger dildo, not the giant, too-big-for-any-kind-of-purpose one but the one that is the perfect imitation of his own cock. His head is pinned against the bed; his eyes are closed. Sweat gathers at his collarbone. His nipples are large and moist. As you move the larger dildo in and out of his ass you fill your free hand with more lubricant. You rub this onto his cock and his body shudders to accept your touch. His eyes look down again at you briefly and blink in your presence, noting you are still wearing the plastic gloves.

As you move your hands in and out, up and down, he shudders again and comes.

o   o   o

If he were any less handsome he would have lost a lot of points by now. He would lose points for falling asleep after you pulled the dildo out. He would lose a lot more points for not helping you clean up.

While you are in the bathroom washing his dildos you realize there is no stench at all in this room. His bathroom is large and perfect, just like his room. His bathroom is not on top of a septic tank. Maybe this was all arranged beforehand. Maybe the sleepy-eyed clerk is in on this. Maybe the sleepy-eyed clerk expected him to call room service so that he could show up at the door and offer some kind of service. *Go ahead,* you think. *This one is all yours. He didn't even care if I took off my clothes. Go ahead, take what you can. Give what you've got to give. He's all yours if you want him.*

While you're putting your jeans on you have another glass of wine and then finish the glass that he started. He is still sleeping. He looks like the kind of guy you would only someday hope to look at like this in a room like this one. You consider staying and just watching him sleep, but when you realize that he is snoring you decide to go back to your own room. You gather up the stained blue shirt and the bottle of wine and softly close the door behind you.

Back in your room you realize the wine has started to have an effect on you. Your mind moves from one image to the next. They are all of him. They are all of him on the bed with one of your hands grasping a dildo and the other hand grasping the real thing. You are a part of the picture but not entirely seen. It is his ass, his cock, his dildo that mesmerizes you.

When you are undressed you realize that the pleasure has been all his tonight. You never came. You never had an orgasm. He never even cared that you didn't come. Any other man would lose a big chunk of points for this (and most usually do), but this man, you realize, has given you something that you cannot quite shake from your head. You sort through the images in your mind of his ass, his cock, his dildos, and your hands and find the one you need. Blood surges through you once more. This heightened sense makes you realize that the stench of the bathroom has now invaded your room. You take the beautiful blue stained shirt and press it against your nose. You come easily, overwhelmed by the sense of being near something that has been so near to him for such a long time.

o   o   o

In the morning it is raining. When you meet him for breakfast in the lodge restaurant you agree to drive back early. You have no desire to traipse around the mountain in the rain and mud, and you would rather be in your tiny apartment in the city by yourself than alone in a tiny, smelly room in the country.

You are fully prepared to sit in silence for the entire drive back to the city. While he is just as handsome today as he was the day before this miserable, rainy one, you have no desire to open a channel of communication with him. He begins the drive with the radio on, but since he is in a bright, chipper mood, despite the rain, he wants to talk, so he turns the music down low.

"Have you been with a lot of married men?" he asks you.

His question startles you and you struggle with your thoughts before you supply him with an answer. You are not sure if he means if you knew the men before him were married when you had sex with them or if you consciously had sex with them because they were married. You realize the answer, "Yes," would work in both cases. "A few," you tell him, though you do not provide him with any more details. You try to calculate the number of married men you have slept with and lose count because you keep remembering a few you are certain were separated at the time. You decide the best way out of this miserable internal counting game is to turn the topic of conversation back to him.

"When did you know you were gay?" you ask.

The question frightens him. You can tell this by the way he grins.

"I mean, were you already married? Or did you know it before and hope that being married would make it disappear?"

He clearly does not want to answer you. He pretends to look at the traffic on the road, the way the rain is falling. He slows down the car, grips the steering wheel with both hands. "I could never do what you do," he says.

His answer is vague and you struggle with whether he has insulted you or not. Something in the next few seconds makes you realize that he would never admit to being gay. It is no surprise when the next sentence out of his mouth is, "I could never leave my wife. Or my kids."

The rain continues. The windshield wipers flip back and forth. You decide you are enjoying his discomfort. For the first time this weekend you feel in control of the situation. "But which do you prefer?" you ask him. "Sex with guys or sex with women?"

"It's not that black or white with me," he says.

"What do you mean?" you ask him. "You have a mistress too?"

When he doesn't answer you realize that of course he does. Of course this too handsome gorgeous man takes everything that comes his way. Even his next answer, "I see a few women, too," doesn't surprise you, though it disappoints you. Terribly, terribly disappoints you.

The balance has again shifted into his lap. Of course he sees women. Of course that explains everything. He has sex with women and you are a bag of festering germs who sleeps in a separate bed. You try not to feel insulted when he says, "It really depends on the person. I know it's really shallow but I'm attracted to the way a person looks, not whether it is a guy or a girl. I can just tell by the way someone looks who's worth spending time with and who's not. Or at least I hope I can tell. That's why I thought we would get along."

You are not sure if he has insulted you again. But his tone, like that of a parent scolding a child, makes you feel lousy. You look out at the rain, then press your forehead against the window. The conversation is over. The music grows louder. You feel a headache begin. Someone, someone above you—yes, that giant puppeteer is back and in the miserable gray sky above—wants you to find out one more thing. He will not let you close your eyes until you know it. "Have you ever had a boyfriend before?" you ask. Your voice bounces against the window and slices through the music.

His answer is low, soft, and you have no idea what he is saying. You have no desire to ask him to repeat it. Instead, you look out at the rain and then close your eyes. You realize you are very, very sleepy. When you wake sometime later the suburbs are growing more dense, the buildings are taller; the highway stretches around another and into another. The radio blinks on and off when you enter the tunnel.

When the car stops at the point where he picked you up the day before, he asks, "You have an umbrella?"

"Somewhere," you answer.

"I can call you in a few days," he says. "We could get together again."

Before you open the door you take another look at him. Yes, he is right, you can tell things about a person by the way they look. You can tell exactly who and what they are. Or are not. And what they could mean to you. "Okay," you answer and before you know it you are on the sidewalk facing a new set of choices. Do you look for your umbrella buried in your bag or do you just walk in the rain?

No contest, you decide. You start walking.

What Do You Call This?

You cannot watch this happen. You squeeze his hand, use the pressure as a sign to communicate with him. His response is no response at all. His fingers twitch. His body shakes. His breathing sounds like wind trying to find its way through a forest.

His face no longer belongs to him, the thin, startled expression borrowed from a horror movie you watched decades before as a kid. His body no longer belongs to a thirty-two year old, reduced to a yeasty tumble of skin and bones. You cannot stay and watch this any longer. You say to him: "Keith, I have to leave for a minute." You let go of his hand, flee to the hall.

The nurse has left her clipboard on a cart outside the room. You glance at a column of times and entries, notes about when he was last cleaned, what medications were given, which ones will be next. From the doorway of the room you watch her turn Keith on his side to help him breathe. While you watch her struggle with his twitching hand, you can hear your own breathing. You sound like a truck with bad breaks screeching to a halt.

"I thought you were going to help me," Keith said to you two weeks ago.

"So I'm a coward," you answered, matter-of-factly. You were helping him brush his teeth. He was spitting into a pan you held beneath his chin.

"You said you loved me," he said, the minty smell of his words hitting your nose.

"I did," you answered. "I do."

"Then why won't you help me?" he asked.

You have helped him write his will, give away his porn, tell his mother he was sick. You have even helped him plan his memorial, writing lists of songs and readings and names of friends who should speak and sing. "I've helped you with plenty," you told him. "I'm not going to help you kill yourself."

"Then you don't love me," he said. "If you love me, you'll help me do it."

"No," you answered him swiftly. "I don't want to let you go."

o   o   o

He had had outlined how to do it without you. In the hospital he told you he had gotten both Compazine and Nembutal, like the way it had been done in a book he had read. You knew it had been on his mind long before he brought it up. Once, months ago, when you met him at his apartment before going out to see a movie, you noticed a pamphlet from the Hemlock Society sitting on his bookshelf.

This was weeks before the pain in his legs began. Or, rather, weeks before he confessed the pain to you. There was always some kind of lapse between his thinking about something, his acceptance of what was happening, and letting the admission break free. His pride kept a lot of details hidden until the night he lost it in front of you. You were seated at a table in an expensive restaurant. He was treating because he had gotten a raise, or said he had gotten a raise but you know now he did not, that he was only charging up his credit card, convinced he would never have to pay. While eating crepes his face went pale. His lips and cheeks drew back like he was going to sneeze. Then he leaned over and threw up on the floor.

"I've heard a lot of stories like that," the nurse said to you when you told her this one night while he was sleeping. "One boy just went in front of my eyes. A fever killed him in minutes."

o   o   o

"He's a strong young man," a doctor tells you in the hall. The nurse has summoned him and you wait outside the room while the examination takes place. "It's very natural for his body to want to fight. He could last a long time."

"Like this?"

"Eventually..." the doctor says, not completing his sentence. "He's been weakened. But it might be some time."

"How long?" you ask.

"I can't really say," he answers. "His body is still fighting. The machine would keep the breathing going."

It is late; so late it is really early morning. Keith's mother and his older sister Emily have returned to the suburbs, to another country, far away from this hospital room. "Is he in any kind of pain?" you ask.

"There's a drip going," says the doctor. "So it's hard to say how much he really feels."

"Does he know what's happening?"

"There's still brain activity," the doctor says. "There are theories that he retains some forms of sensation."

"Theories?" you echo.

The doctor does not respond except to stand firmly in front of you, blocking your view of the room. To look at Keith, in the hospital bed, struggling to breathe, you would have to step around him. He was only admitted to repair the catheter implanted in his chest. The stitching had fallen out. This wasn't supposed to happen. He was supposed to be getting better. Not weaker.

"It's your decision," the doctor says and hides his hands in the pockets of his white jacket.

"He wanted to be at home," you say. "This is not the way he wanted it to happen."

o   o   o

How did this happen? Four years ago you had seen the matinee of a play together and were on your way to dinner. You followed him into a drug store where he stopped in front of the stationery aisle and lifted a piece of paper from a rack. A co-worker wanted one, he said to you holding up the sheet. Tony was sick. His boyfriend Greg had died. "I might as well get one for myself," Keith said. "You want one too?"

You had no idea what he was holding, what he was doing. When you looked at the paper you said, "No. Not at all."

"I'm naming you," he said, the way someone would tick off an item found on a grocery store list.

"Let's not talk about it," you said.

"It's what I want," he answered.

No cardiac resuscitation, no mechanical respiration, no tube feeding, no antibiotics. Maximum pain relief. Keith handed it to you two weeks ago, when things were getting worse.

It read: In case of an incurable or irreversible mental or physical condition with no reasonable expectation of recovery. Permanently unconscious, irreversible brain damage, unable to make his own decisions.

This power doesn't belong to you. Why should you have to play God? Why should you have to play God when God has stopped the game? How did this happen? Why did you let yourself fall in love with a dying man?

o o o

When he was six, his mother told you, he had jumped from the second story window of their house. He thought he could fly. Like Peter Pan. Both legs were broken in the fall and the setback did not make him any older or wiser, or so she said. "He was always a bit too adventurous," she said earlier today. "When he was eight he swatted down a bee's nest and we had to rush him to the hospital."

You told her he was a lot like your older brother, always getting into trouble. When you were seven and he was eleven, he caught a squirrel and kept him in a cage in the basement until one night you went down and set him free. The next year, when he wounded a bird, you would have set the bird free too had your sister's cat not killed it first.

This last story reminds you of the absence of God. You had cried when you discovered the crushed remains of the bird on the basement floor.

o   o   o

It happened after the restaurant, the sudden confession in the cab back to his apartment. "I was tested last year," he said. "The medicine makes me sick."

He came to rely on you for little things: first, advice: Should I go in for a transfusion? Should I have a spinal tap? Then, to help get items from his shopping list: protein shakes, more Kleenex, some frozen fruit on a stick because it didn't upset the stomach. You came to need hearing him every day, how things were going, what he thought was causing the pain in his lower left back, what might be creating the sudden, burning headaches. Your questions drew you closer. His stories sealed the bond. He talked about the trip he had made to Egypt two years before, the fight he had with his boyfriend of the time, a man he refused to name. You compared worst dates. "Yes," he said. "Yours are pretty bad. On that matter, I'll concede. You win on the all-time worst dates."

o   o   o

Earlier this afternoon, you had lunch with his sister in the hospital cafeteria.

"I don't understand why he didn't tell us earlier," Emily said.

"I'm sure he didn't want you to worry," you said.

"But that's what family does," she answered. "We are supposed to worry about each other. We are supposed to take care of each other. We are supposed to know about this so we can help him."

First, you noticed how much her anger looked like his. Then,

49

you thought there was nothing she could do. Nothing he would have wanted her to do.

"It's just like him to keep it a secret," she said. "I never met any of his friends before this happened. It's just like him to keep me out of his life."

o   o   o

His friends became your friends. Tony. Greg. Simon. Clay. Jerry. Peter said he kept his friends distant, isolated, segregated. "Everyone but you," Peter said. "Why was that?"

"You met them all at the circus benefit," you said to him.

"No, not Tony," he said. "Nor Greg."

"Greg was sick," you explained. "That's why he wasn't there."

"He never wanted us to meet," Peter said. "I heard stories about Greg all the time. He loved to talk about the way Tony would act in the office with a client. I never even met Clay. Hell, I didn't even know about Clay until it was over."

Clay was the last guy Keith dated, or the last guy he admitted to dating, though you know for a fact that Keith continued to go out on the nights they didn't spend together, still searching for a guy who was always not right, or so he liked to explain, so it would be easy for him to move on to the next one, the next perfectly imperfect man.

In your mind you were all alike. All of his friends. You had *him* in common. Simon had tricked with Keith at the baths downtown and then had become friends. Jerry and Keith had been boyfriends in college. Keith had joined Tony and Greg for threesomes, which was how he got hooked up with the job in a press office (and another story that Peter was never told because Peter was, in Keith's mind, still an ex-boyfriend). Peter was the first of Keith's boyfriends you ever met, though Keith never discovered what happened between you and Peter in Atlantic City. Or maybe he did and never told you. Never let you know that he knew. Somehow you had managed to turn your own one night stand with Keith into a friendship, though you are not exactly sure how. Movies, maybe. Or the theater. You always thought he asked you out when nobody else was available.

And you were both the same age. That helped the friendship, too. Born, you learned the night you slept with him, four months and nine hundred miles apart.

o   o   o

Once, when he was sleeping, you read the diary he scribbled in throughout the day and you noticed your absence from the daily routine of his life. You expected his writings to be full of confessions, regrets, theories, tirades. Instead, it was a list of details from which you were absent. "I dozed fitfully for an hour or so," he wrote one day two months before, "then made clam chowder and watched *Another World*." There were mentions of a trip to the post office, a haircut in a friend's office, episodes of *I Love Lucy* and *The Avengers*. But no mention of the afternoon you took off from work because he needed help getting to his doctor's office. You wondered if the meaning you were investing in caring for him was one-sided; if he had said, "I love you" the afternoon you brought him home from the hospital because he was vulnerable and it was a more generous way of saying "thank you."

He said it again the night you stayed over instead of returning to your own apartment. In bed with him, you couldn't fall asleep, worrying as you wrapped your arms around him that you would become entangled in the IV tubing that fed him through a vein in his arm. Days later, when you read the diary, again there was no mention of those three words. Nor the fact that you were now sleeping at the foot of his bed, on the floor on top of a pile of blankets, ready to help in the middle of the night because it meant dragging the IV unit to the bathroom behind him.

Was it love when he let you hold him steady while he peed or when you cleaned up the trail of shit he left because of constant diarrhea? Was it *because* of love that you did this for him? Was this love when you gathered his used tissues or scraped his half-chewed food into the trash? It was true there was something deeper going on, something fearful, spiritual, hopeful, and thankful. It was certainly the most intimate moments you had ever shared with someone, though there was nothing at all sexual to any of this. Sex had long evaporated from your relationship with him, even the aftertales of bar-hopping and anonymous tricks had become a thing of the past—nostalgia, recalled like a favorite song you had heard over and over on the radio in junior high.

What would you call this then? Something more than friendship, something less than lovers? What was it now, watching him in a hospital bed fighting to breathe, wishing his body would give up and ease your own conscience? Of course he is going to die. But did you want this decision to haunt you the rest of your life? So what do you call *this*? Love? Suicide? Murder? An act of mercy or an act of love? Something you will not forget?

o   o   o

You were better when you had something to do: bringing him the mail, helping him into a clean T-shirt, changing the bag of fluids hanging on the pole. This waiting, this doctor telling you again that the surgery to repair the catheter is no longer possible, makes you crazy, angry, anxious.

"You must hate me for doing this to you," he said last week.

"Of course not," you answered, though you hated the guilt you felt for being well; the lying to his friends, his mother, his sister, even *him*. Telling him that he was getting better, that he looked like he had put on weight, that there was nothing wrong with the way his hair looked, even though he had less of it and what he had had no color. Like his skin. And lips. And eyes: puzzled pools of nothing but need.

You wouldn't have been this strong if this were you in bed, struggling to breathe. You would have jumped, swallowed the pills, plunged a razor across your wrists, held your breath under water until you couldn't hold it anymore.

"We can't go on like this," he said when you brought him back to the hospital three days ago. You dismissed his concern, telling him to listen to what the doctor would say. This was not at all expected. *He was supposed to get better.* Even when his mother left this afternoon she did not expect it was time to say good-bye. *Good-bye. It was not time to say good-bye.*

In the hallway, waiting, you are suddenly consumed: What if he dies without me? Without me there? To see it. To hold his hand. To help him, guide him, comfort him. You leave the doctor in the hall, walk back to the room, up to the chair beside the bed and sit down, leaning into the stench of his breath. The muscles of his face flicker through a series of expressions you recognize after knowing him, what, all these eight years—the eyebrows tilting in surprise, the nose pinching itself smaller with worry, the corners of his mouth containing his anger. He knows you are back beside him. Somehow, unconscious, he knows you are here. He senses you. *You.* Not someone else. You are now his family, the one he is leaving behind.

o   o   o

You find his sister's number in your backpack. You will call her first. She will call his mother, will pass the decision on. No, you are not exactly family, either, are you? You cannot tell his mother, *"Your son is dying and he wants me to kill him."* Life is not supposed to be that brutal and honest, not even in death. While you are dialing you rehearse the words you will say to his sister, the exact phrasing, putting them in one order and then in another. "This is what he wanted," you practice. "This is what he wrote. What he decided. It's not my decision, this is his. This is what he wanted, what he wrote."

The phone rings and you wait for an answer. When Emily answers you notice her voice is soft, groggy, that you have woken her up to tell her bad news. You think about hanging up without saying your name, saying anything, though she will know it is you, why you have called because you *are* a part of his family now. You are a part of this pain. She knows this, doesn't she? This is why she is angry, too.

You wait, waiting for her to recognize your silence. "Emily," you finally say. "There is something I must tell you."

What You Talk About

You have made arrangements to meet him at a bar.s He answered the personal ad which you placed. When you talked on the phone with him he seemed nice and interested in you, but so did the other two blind dates you had this week. Upon meeting them you found that one was balding and the other wore an earring in his left ear. Not that this really bothered you, you have dated men before with both those characteristics. But the first one had the mannerisms of a truck driver and the appearance of a nerd, the second looked like the type of person you would avoid in dark alleys. And what really did bother you was you could not connect with them no matter how hard you tried, they were both so vague, one was even mysterious. The minute you got home from the second blind date you called to arrange the third. You were a little drunk because you had a beer on an empty stomach and as you described yourself over the phone you heard yourself slur a few words.

You are meeting this third date at a bar you have never been to. Your expectations are not high and you are a little stressed out from the previous dates and a tough week at a job you don't much like. It is Friday night. The arrangements you made were only for a drink; dinner together following was an option either party could refuse. However you are already hungry. As you enter the bar you hope for a moment you have been stood up.

There are only two men in this bar. One you estimate is over sixty-five. You know it is not him. In the light of this bar, which is dim, the other man looks quite handsome; virile and rugged, like the type riding a horse in a cigarette ad. You try to wipe the shock from your face as he turns to you and speaks your name.

You wonder how he recognized you. You worry a minute about whether you look too gay as he shakes your hand; after all, this is a straight bar. Then you remember you told him you wore black wire rim eyeglasses. No one else in the bar is wearing black wire rim eyeglasses.

As he rises from the bar stool where he was seated you see he is shorter than you expected. Though he told you he was six feet tall, he does not seem four inches taller than you. Perhaps it is because one of your earlier dates this week also described himself as six feet tall, but he was in actuality six feet two inches tall. The man tonight also appears heavier than you expected, not chubby but solid. Perhaps this is because the earlier tall date was one hundred-fifty pounds. This six foot guy told you he was one hundred sixty-six. He looks healthy, you notice. He has a full head of hair and no earring. You observe right away that he has large hands and small feet. You sit down on a bar stool and worry because you think your feet are larger proportionally than your hands. He sits down beside you and places his hand against his beer bottle. You order a beer: lite, low calorie.

There is an awkward pause after your first sip of beer. The carbonation in your mouth and stomach has jolted your senses. You cough and look at the bartender, a short, husky man with closely cropped black hair peppered with gray and admire the way the tendons of his arms flex as he wipes the inside of a glass with a cloth. You think that the bartender is not better looking than this guy. Your blind date asks if you had any trouble finding this bar. No, you answer, only finding a parking space on this block. You ended up parking on a side street. There is another awkward pause. You look around the bar and say this is a nice place, you never knew it existed. He says he has only been here a few times and points to a doorway that leads to a restaurant. He says it is rather expensive. Another awkward pause and he asks you how your week was. A strange question to ask, you think, because at the beginning of this week he did not even know you. Rough, you answer, and begin to complain about the woman you work for and the hour it takes to commute to your job. You start to describe your car, an old relic, which you are convinced personally dislikes you because it keeps having to be repaired, when you realize you are complaining too much. You ask him how his day was, but your voice sounds edgy. It doesn't sound as sincere as when he asked his question. While he tells you he got up early this morning to finish a few errands and do some cleaning before leaving for work, you notice he sounds calm, as though all his thoughts are carefully organized before he speaks. His voice is light and fluid; you cannot detect any accent. When you mention you saw a tiny field mouse run across your bathroom carpet this morning he laughs, and you like the way it ends in a quick, raspy crack. He says he was busy at work and adds he got home around four o'clock and took a nap before coming here tonight. No wonder he seems so at ease, you think. No wonder he looks so good. No wonder he doesn't look bitter, angry, or depressed. He had a nap.

What you know about him already: He wrote you he does not smoke or do drugs. He is a teacher. Like you he is in his early thirties and he is looking for a friend and/or lover. He likes to go bowling and refinish furniture and considers himself conservative. During the first phone conversation you had with him he told you he has a cat, lives in a third floor apartment, doesn't go out to bars much unless with a friend, and was reading *Significant Others* when you called. Enough to convince you he was not an ax murderer.

You ask him what subject he teaches. He says botany. You ask if that is a requirement for a high school diploma in this state. He answers that it is a special course for advanced students. While he is explaining the course he teaches you are thinking about the cottage you are renting. You had heard that the previous tenants were amateur horticulturists. In your yard there are several plants surrounded by wire or propped up by long, thin stakes. You wonder how to work this into the conversation. You don't when you realize you don't know the names of any of these plants, and you are attracted to this guy, he interests you, and you don't want to turn him off by seeming ignorant.

He asks you if you grew up in this area. You tell him you are originally from the South and after college you moved to New York City where you lived for ten years. You say you never even realized this state existed until you visited last summer with a friend who was looking to buy a weekend house. You tell him you have only lived here for three months. The only people you know are your friend and his lover who bought a house, the real estate agent who sold it to them, and a lesbian couple who run an inn nearby. You don't tell him the reason why you moved out of Manhattan. You don't mention that everything about the city was beginning to annoy you, your job made you irritable, and you hated watching your best friend Keith die from AIDS. You only say you needed a change. You try to keep the conversation light. You tell him it is so different living in a rural area. You mention you just learned how to clean your chimney. You add you never realized you would spend so much time scraping frost off your windshield.

He tells you he has lived here for three years. Before that he was in North Carolina and Ohio and California. He asks you if you have dated much. You wonder what the term date means this year and in this part of the country. Does it mean date as in getting together with a friend, date as in one person pays for everything two people do, or date as it was known in the Seventies, to have sex. You opt for the last choice since he is your age, and you realize your answer really fits all three definitions: not much.

You notice he is staring at you. Looking you over. You think at last all those mornings you spend exercising are finally paying off. You know you look younger than your stated age. All your friends tell you so, even your other blind dates this week mentioned the fact that you could pass for someone in their mid-twenties. The first date told you your eyes were extraordinary, the way the light green irises were circled by a dark olive band. The other mentioned the way you described yourself in your ad was an understatement; he never anticipated meeting someone so good-looking. You wonder if your date notices the tiny nick in the cleft of your chin where you cut yourself shaving this morning. He asks you if you go out to the bars much. You say you did when you first moved here, because you thought you might meet someone. Then you tell him you haven't been to them in a while because you realized they are packed with out-of-towners, men available for only a night. You tell him you want a more permanent situation, which is why you placed the ad.

He is wearing a heavy knit maroon sweater, but you can tell he keeps himself in shape by the way the fabric stretches across his shoulders. You imagine what he looks like undressed, though you cannot determine whether his chest is hairy or smooth. You decide it must be smooth, because you do not notice any hair at his wrists, and though you remind yourself you must be interested in the person, not the physique, you cannot shake the mental photograph you have created of the two of you in bed together, your head resting on top of his smooth chest. You wonder if he likes to kiss, cuddle, wrestle or massage. He looks briefly at you and then glances in the direction of the bartender. You know he is making a comparison. He turns again toward you and you study his expression, looking for some sort of sign of disappointment, but he smiles at you and takes a sip of his beer. You wonder what sex would be like with him. Is he rough or passionate, gentle or affectionate? You begin to twirl the bottom of the beer bottle between the palms of your hands, a habit you have when you are nervous. You wonder if he knows what you are thinking. You wonder when was the last time he had sex.

When you spoke with him on the phone you told him you are hard-working and honest, stable but shy, which is why you are never relaxed at a bar. You said you are easily entertained and consider yourself a romantic. You mentioned you are both rational and adventurous, intelligent and athletic, and have a dry, sometimes cynical sense of humor. You said you like traveling, reading magazines and playing the piano, enjoy the theater, photography, and biking. You told him you watch your weight, eat plenty of fiber, and keep your light brown hair short and trimmed regularly. You added you are a casual dresser, choosing clothes for comfort, though tonight you are wearing the indigo shirt that makes your eyes look softer, bluer. You notice you are both wearing jeans, though his are a new blue and yours are an old black. You make a mental note of what you are wearing. If you see this guy again you must not wear the same outfit.

He asks you if you went home for the holidays. You say no because you were just there in September for your youngest sister's wedding. You say this matter of factly, without any emotion, exactly the way you said it to your two previous dates this week. You think your tone sounded a little too blunt so you add that your parents' house in Atlanta was too far to drive with only one day off so you spent the holiday with a friend and her mother who lives in Connecticut. There is an awkward pause. You notice his expression, which you think looks serious. You think this is too much information for him to register at once. Then he says his sister is expecting a baby any time now. She lives in Florida and he explains his mother spent the holidays down there this year. You think a moment about Florida and the sun and the beach and the hot weather.

You ask him if he thinks it is going to snow this weekend. He says they are predicting four to six inches. You remember you have just spent a fortune to have snow tires put on your car. You ask him how the roads are here when it snows. He says they are pretty good about plowing the main ones, but the back roads can be difficult.

You have finished your beer. He takes the last sip of his. He asks if you want to have dinner. He's interested, you think, and you answer yes. He asks where you want to eat. You remember you don't have a lot of money in your wallet. You suggest a place three blocks away, a restaurant that has a comfortable, homey feel: dark, unpretentious, and inexpensive. You slip on your jacket and head for the door.

Outside you walk slightly ahead of him. The sidewalk is narrow and since you are the one who knows where the restaurant is, you lead the way. When you arrive at the building, you hold the door open for him to enter first. Inside, you watch him mentally take in the surroundings.

A blond waiter shows you to a table. Looking at the menu your blind date asks you what you recommend. You say the chicken and veal are good but you will probably order something light like the chef salad. You think to yourself that this appears healthy and when you ordered it once before, you couldn't finish it. You don't want to appear piggish.

The waiter brings glasses of water and takes your order. Your blind date opts for the chicken. You stick with the salad. When the waiter leaves your date asks if you think the waiter is cute. You say sort of and mention that if he had shaved and showered this morning he could probably be a knockout. He says he has a weakness for blonds. You feel like you've lost a race. You wonder what you would look like if you dyed your hair.

The lighting is brighter in the restaurant than it was at the bar. You notice for the first time your blind date has brown eyes. There is a small bend at the bridge of his nose. You wonder if it was ever broken. You want to ask him to come over tonight. Instead you ask him what his plans are for the weekend.

He tells you he has some work to do on Saturday and then adds he is having brunch on Sunday with some friends. He asks if you like to cook. You answer only if it's frozen. You have little patience for chopping, stirring, browning, and all that stuff. He says he enjoys cooking. You think he holds the invention of the microwave against you. He asks what type of food you like to eat. You say just about anything, but your all-time favorite food is pineapple upside-down cake. He says he likes vegetables a lot. What type of vegetables do you like? he asks. You feel an urge to roll your eyes but you suppress it. Again you feel defeated. You are thirty-three years old and you are being judged by your interest in vegetables. Anything, you answer. Except lima beans. You wrinkle your nose. It is an ingrained reflex. You instantly regret your answer. There is only one other word in the English language which produces that same expression on your face and that word is liver. And though you don't mention that, you can't keep from thinking about it. He says he likes lima beans.

You try to redeem yourself by saying your mother was not a good cook. You explain to him how over the years you have developed a taste for things slightly charred. You know instinctively this conversation is headed in the wrong direction. There is an awkward pause. You panic that you have lost him. You change the subject. You ask him if he saw the new Bette Midler movie. He says he hasn't been to a movie in about four months. You are thankful when the waiter reappears with your food.

You talk sporadically while you eat. You offer him your onions which he accepts. He offers you a taste of his chicken which you decline because you are not in the mood for chicken. But then you worry he might be offended you didn't accept—you remember someone once told you that sharing food is an intimate gesture—so you tell him you changed your mind, you will try a piece. You watch him slice off a corner of a thigh and place it onto your plate. You wonder what it would be like sitting down to dinner every night with this man. Would you like what he cooks, would your plates match his glasses, could you afford to live in a place that has a built-in dishwasher? You wonder if he is neat or sloppy. Does he leave the cap off the toothpaste, forget to flush, wash colors and whites together, remember to take the trash out on Wednesdays? You hope he wouldn't object to your favorite towel, the old, unraveling, large dark green one.

He asks if you have had a lot of responses to your ad. You say only a few but you do not mention your other dates this week. He says he is sort of seeing another guy, but the guy is more interested in him than he is in this guy. You think: Isn't that the way it always works?

You have finished dinner and have ordered a cup of coffee, decaffeinated. You are frantically racking your brain so you can make some sort of connection with this man. He asks you what type of music you listen to. You say you enjoy everything except heavy metal. You tell him what you listen to is usually determined by your mood. You like oldies during the week, Top 40 and disco on Saturdays, and classical, preferably baroque, on Sundays. You also explain that you usually like a particular song more than an artist which is why you haven't bought any albums in a long time. He says he likes country music a lot. You say you like the way country music has evolved over the last few years. The way the lyrics have matured. You say you like country music a lot more since you no longer live in the South. He says his favorite singer is Patsy Cline. You agree, Patsy Cline is unbeatable.

You split the bill and leave the waiter a generous tip, in spite of the fact he was a distracting blond. Outside, the night air feels refreshing and you walk together in the direction of your car. You realize you have done too much talking and thinking tonight and you are tired. But nothing has been said about what you left behind in the city or what changes in his life have caused him to seek a new boyfriend. You like this guy not only because he's attractive but because he is someone who is different from you. You are not a perfect blend, but you feel comfortable enough with him and you think you can learn something from him, something you think is important, looking at the world in a different way.

When you reach your car, you suddenly remember you have never given him your phone number. You don't want to seem pushy about getting together another time. You want him to make the next move, to see if he is interested in you. At your car he asks if you want to get together again next week. You say yes and write your name on a piece of paper you find in your glove compartment. You hand him your number and you both stand awkwardly on the sidewalk. You say, "It was nice to meet you, Bryan." There is no attempt at a kiss; this is a small town after all. You shake hands and he says, "I'll call you soon."

In the car driving home you wonder if he will ever call. You think again about your friend Keith and miss him, deeply. And then you think again about vegetables. You wish you had told Bryan you really like spinach. You have always liked spinach. You will always like spinach.

What is Enough?

He thinks you have incredible buns.

You like the tight flatness of his stomach.

He cups his mouth around your chin and you feel his tongue wet the morning stubble of your beard. He is lying on top of you. You run your hands down his back, tapping the knots of his spine like the keys of a piano. You press your face against his neck, detecting scents of grass and tarragon and Perry Ellis cologne buried beneath the dark, wiry hairs of his chest. He brushes his cheek against yours and you smell his breath, sour and bitter as burnt chocolate, but surprisingly fragrant and arousing to you because you know it as one of his morning smells. He shifts his body a fraction lower so that his sternum presses against yours, and the abrasion and then sudden stillness of skin against skin makes your chest become moist with sweat and your armpits and brow itch as the heat of him, the fever of his flesh, engulfs you. He lifts himself up and rolls over on his back. The bedsheet follows him and twists around your left leg so that you are pinned in an awkward position. As you turn over to wrap your arms around his waist and kick your leg free the sun catches in your eyes and you squint. He pushes you back on your back and uses your body as a pillow, folding one arm beneath your neck and stretching the other across your thigh, curling his body so that it bends around you. You comb your fingers through the short black strands of his hair and then stroke the back of his neck while looking up at the ceiling—dark timbers slanting skyward to make a frame which cracks and creaks like the joints of an old man. You think you might love this man, this one feels different than the others: more magnetic, seductive, sensual. The one just before him, the one you loved not too long ago, annoyed you, irritated you, baffled and confused you. Your body becomes rigid for a moment as you wonder if this one will someday say he loves you.

Looking at him, you notice he has closed his eyes. You think he wants to go back to sleep so you wedge yourself from underneath him. When you reach the edge of the bed he grabs you from behind and begins to kiss the back of your neck. You arch your back as he works his lips around your right shoulder. He slips his hand through the hairs of your chest, rubbing your skin, finally settling two fingers against a nipple and dialing as though fine-tuning a radio. He rubs your chest again, harder, and you feel a lightness, like a startled bird, flush up into your lungs. You slide around in his grasp and kiss him lightly on the forehead; as you do, your bodies slowly bend back to the bed. Now you are on top of him and you kiss, in sequence, his eyebrows, eyelashes, nose, cheeks, and chin before your lips meet his. Again you notice his breath is warm and bitter and when your tongue enters his mouth you feel it slide against his upper teeth. You relax your body even more, stretching out on top of his.

He places his hands on your shoulders and gently begins to massage the muscles of your back. Again you notice the solidness of his actions. He works his fingers deeply, separating and manipulating each tendon. As you lean your head against his shoulder, your eyes buried into the pillow, you think again about Bryan, the man before this one. Bryan was always hesitant, his glances unsure, uncertain if he even wanted to be with you. He never liked being touched, never enjoyed being embraced. This man, Ross, has no such confusions. He seems to you to be the type of man who never sleeps alone; if he weren't with you, there would be another. You think about your life before Ross, before Bryan, what it was like sleeping alone, waking up in the morning in a bed by yourself. You were not unhappy then, but you were not content, either. You had created your own little world in which to think and live; you were self-sufficient with friends and fantasies. Yet you believed there was a man out there for you somewhere, one who wanted to be with you as much as you wanted to be with him. You never considered yourself particular, all you asked is that the right man be loving and committed. You didn't care if he was taller or shorter, blond or brunet. But you had built bridges across your heart in case you never found him; you had hidden your emotions beneath a functional, businesslike personality so you couldn't be hurt. The last thing that you, a man in his thirties, needed was to have your heart broken. You had enough anxieties from potential viruses and escalating interest rates.

When you first started dating Bryan, you were relieved when you discovered that you shared similarities. You were both from large, religious families, had come out in your early twenties, had an appreciation for music and a desire to travel. You were excited to have met someone you liked and who liked you as much in return. In fact, he became your friend before you had sex together. When he began to stay overnight at your apartment you were wildly alert, unable to sleep. You were not used to another body beside you in bed. You were not used to sharing blankets, sheets, pillows, and a limited cubic space. You worried whether your tossing and turning prevented him from sleeping. In the mornings you were exhausted, squeezed into positions you would never have found yourself in if you were alone. Later, when you became used to him, used to his smells and sounds and habits, even the way he would turn over on his side and cough to clear his throat, you still could not sleep. You were always disoriented and restless when you slept over at his apartment. At yours, you didn't understand why he seldom held you in bed, were confused why he never made the first advances for sex. You worried he would leave you, if he had met someone else. You wondered if he was attracted to you, had decided he no longer wanted to be with you. You ached for him just to touch you. Now, as Ross's hands work their way down your back and knead your buttocks you understand what a friend once told you was so special about sex, how the human skin needs to be touched. You remember the reason why you decided to be gay: you enjoyed sex with men more than women. Now, though you have only known Ross a few weeks, you are aware you are used to all of him: the bulkiness of his frame, the muskiness of his underarms, his method of nuzzling his unshaven face into the crook of your neck, the way he tries to lift your body away from his and pull you back again, as though doing push-ups in space.

This is the time you think Ross likes you best. It is Sunday morning and he is relaxed, rested, ready for sex. His thoughts are focused entirely on you. When you first began dating Bryan, sex was an issue. You were frightened, had not been with a man in a long time. You set the rules right up front: everything safe. He agreed but his caution was different. He wanted to wait before sleeping with you. He felt it should be "making love" not "having sex." You said you felt it should be spontaneous, something both of you wanted, not something planned. Sex with Bryan was awkward, abrupt, unfulfilling. You feel vibrant just being with Ross. Ross tells you you are handsome, whispers that you are the best sex he has had. And he makes you feel special, like now as he sweeps his face across your stomach. Your feet are tucked between his. He runs his hand up and down your thighs and you feel the roughness of it, thick and dry from working outdoors, and yet when you touch his waist you notice the softness of this part of his skin, supple and tender as a woman's flesh.

Bryan told you his caution, his hesitancy to commit to a relationship, was his way of planting a seed in your heart, weeding and watering it and watching it grow. You told him you were the type that fell in love instantly. You were ruled by instinct, and your instinct was usually right. Once, when Bryan was drunk, he said he didn't love you and maybe never would and you walked out on him, telling yourself you didn't need all this in the first place: you didn't need a one-sided relationship, you didn't need all this frustration and confusion, and you felt sure that by being alone you could now be happy. But he came after you and apologized and was more attentive than before. He called every day and cooked dinner for you, sometimes showing up unannounced at your apartment, unexpectedly taking you out to a movie or to try a new restaurant. He wanted to know everything about you: your past, your personality, your passions. He wanted to spend time with you, get to know you better. It was then that you decided if this was a man who would never be able to say I love you, you would at least find a way to make him need to be with you.

Ross pokes his fingers beneath your arm and tickles you. He knows this drives you crazy. Somewhere between Bryan and Ross you became touch sensitive. You twist yourself away from his hand and push your finger back and forth where his skin touches his pelvis. He wiggles and laughs. This is one of the most sensitive areas of his body. He holds you tighter and your fingers slip to his ribs and again you find another tender, ticklish spot. He jerks away from you and grasps both of your hands by the wrists and pins them against the mattress. Sometimes this playfulness will lead to a wrestling match, one trying to tickle till the other gives in. But this morning he kisses you lightly around the neck, till he works his way up to your lips.

You know his body by heart: his hair, thick, dark waves cascading around a pronounced widow's peak; his shoulders, broad and bony and lightly freckled; his chest, covered with a thick coating of fine black hairs, nipples large and round as quarters; his arms, long and hard, rigid with muscles; his legs, lean and coarse with thicker, tighter strands of hair. Though Ross is five years older than Bryan, in surprisingly better physical shape than Bryan, he has the same difficulty as Bryan in articulating his emotions. But it is easier for you to know what Ross is feeling. You can tell by looking at his face: the sharp, striking cheekbones that lift when he's happy; the almond-shaped eyes that become fine lines when he worries; the slender lips that dimple at the ends when he smiles; the solid line of his jaw when he flexes with anger. He is always in motion, expressing himself physically—gardening, swimming, cleaning, or just eating a piece of fruit. And Ross is always touching you, holding you, draping his arm around your shoulder or your waist, whether alone or in public. And you can remember every time you have had sex together, though you would never tell him you could do so; if you did you would worry whether it would scare him—make him back away from you. With Ross, sex is easy and natural, whether in bed, on the kitchen floor, or in the shower. Sex is the tool he uses to unlock your thoughts, make you throw away your worries. That was not the case with Bryan.

When you first started dating Bryan you gave each other little gifts to express your affection: flowers, a bottle of wine, a deck of playing cards, or a book. You began to collect things that reminded you of the times you spent together: a shell from a beach, a tiny plastic swizzle stick from a cocktail he ordered, a candlestick you pointed to at a flea market. After your third date he asked you if you wanted to date someone else. You said no. He said he liked you because you seemed to be the type of guy who was willing to make a commitment. Since he said that, you have often wondered what it was you tried to commit to; your relationship seemed superficial and shallow, all he wanted was a string of wonderful dates, good times, and nice trips out of town. He wanted to take things slowly; you did not have sex with him until the fifth or sixth date. You slept with Ross the night you met him at a friend's party. All the chemistry and electricity was there with Ross, right at the start.

It still is, but sometimes you feel you know so little about Ross. You don't know what he talks about with his friends. You don't know how he spends his day at work. And Ross knows so little about you. He doesn't know how you got the tiny scar beneath your left eye, doesn't know how many friends you've lost. The first dates you had with Bryan were full of questions; he asked about your family, your job, your earlier boyfriends, your likes and dislikes. And you asked questions of him. Bryan set a standard, both good and bad, you can't ignore. You can't shake off your comparisons; Bryan was much more the romantic—he could spend an evening talking about the future you would share together.

Sometimes you wonder what he is doing now, who Bryan is dating, where he is eating, what he's watching on TV. Sometimes you think you bounced from one man to another too quickly. You were right up front with Ross the night you met him. You told him that you had just split up with a guy and weren't emotionally in any sort of state to start dating. You explained to Ross that night, as you lay in bed together, that Bryan was hesitant about opening up his life to accommodate you. He was protective of his friends, his possessions, his feelings. You became jealous of everything in his life—even of the affection he gave to his cats. But in the end, the reason why you told Bryan that you would never see him again, could not be friends with him, in fact, could never even talk to him again, was because he told you he wanted to see other men. You told him he could date other men but not you at the same time. You told him he had to make a choice, a commitment, one way or the other. He said he liked you, loved you, in fact, but there was no spark, and he needed to see if he could find it with someone else. You grew angry and said you did not find him sexy. He said he was not attracted to you, that you were not his type anyway. There was not a fight. Nothing was left to be said, but the words spoken were too true not to hurt. You were both aggravated because each of you had been desperate to make the relationship work in your own, separate, individual ways.

Ross said you were not the only man with a broken heart. He has had boyfriends and lovers come and go. Some have died. Once, late at night, when he noticed you had been crying, Ross told you he felt your emotions were too large. You told him it was unhealthy to keep everything bottled inside. When you lived alone you worried about bills and how and where to meet a man. When you started dating you worried about bills and how to keep hold of a man. Later, you worried about bills and where that man was when he wasn't with you. Now, Ross thinks you think too much, that too many thoughts are circulating behind your eyes. And he can tell when you are upset, when the thoughts are turning sour. He doesn't have to read your expression or feel for the tension in your body. He knows it intuitively. And when he sees it he smothers you, holding you in his arms till it doesn't matter anymore. He leads you to a subconscious state, a place where no language, questions, or problems exist, till there's not a thought left to think about.

His eyes are open now, as large as dark brown plates before your face. Just when you thought he had moved somewhere inside himself, here he is, looking at you, thinking of you. You slip a hand down his stomach and cup his balls, squeezing them a few times before you start to rub the inside of his thigh. His breath quickens and he begins to kiss you harder; you know he has reached the point where his passion ignites. He buries his head against your chest and begins to lick your left nipple while fingering the indentation of your triceps and twisting his legs around yours. You know he likes your body. You can tell by the way he touches it, strokes it, holds it. You can tell he likes the way your body fits neatly against his, two hard knots of muscle against each other. This is why you continue to do your sit-ups every day, why you go biking and make three trips to the gym every week. He reaches your navel and slides his tongue down to the soft, springy hairs of your groin. You arch your back and twist your hands through his hair. You feel bristly and intense, as though walking through fire. You move by instinct now, your skin feels both pliant and thickened, you can hear your heart pumping violently in your chest. He moves as though weightless, swimming underwater, his body now feels polished and leathery. First he is on top of you, stroking you, then you on him, forcing his arms against the pillow with the palms of your hands as you rock your hips together, the friction making him both smile and moan. Just when you sense he is about to come you back away, teasing him. He gasps and lunges for you and you both roll over onto your sides. You push him onto his back again and when you hold his cock you feel as powerful as a magician suspending a willing victim in midair. He squirms as you move your fist up and down, stops, tenses his body, and holds his breath. You know he has disconnected entirely from you. A warm, pearly-white liquid spills over your fingers. He exhales heavily several times and you rub your hand against his stomach. There's a moment in which you are both silent and still, then he rolls over and is on top of you, his knees straddling your hips. He reaches for your cock and slowly strokes it. You drift in and out of a dream-like state. He starts moving his hand faster; you begin breathing through your mouth. Finally, the motion is so overpowering, you tilt your neck and thrust the back of your head against the bed. He relaxes his grip and you go simultaneously blind and deaf, your thoughts disappear as he lifts you into an orgasm.

You hear him turn on the water for the shower. You roll over and clutch a pillow, sliding it beneath your chest. You take a deep breath and you smell him still beside you. As you shift your weight you feel relaxed but empty, your stomach suddenly cold and wet, your body detached from your mind. You slip your feet beneath the sheet and twist them together, searching for some lingering warmth of him. You think a moment about being all that someone wants. Is Ross enough for you? Could it happen this time? Is this what you *want* or what you *need*?

And then you roll over and close your eyes, wondering if you could convince yourself you could be enough for Ross.

What You Feel

The pain is back, stretching down your neck and across your shoulders. You take a deep breath and tense your back. Releasing the muscles, you feel a momentary relief. But then the pain is back, sharper than ever. You rotate your shoulders. When you stop, the pain is still there. You press your hands against the back of your neck and massage with your fingers. Two days ago, you voluntarily stopped the medication the doctor had prescribed for your anxiety because you felt dull, senseless. Now you wish you hadn't thrown the pills away. Your back feels as if someone is clenching their fist around your spine. The pain is back, and you want it to go away.

You lie on the floor of your apartment, your face facing the ceiling. You close your eyes and take deep, slow breaths. Yesterday at the gym when you had finished your third set of bench presses, just when you had thought you had worked out all the frustration you were carrying inside yourself, just when you hit that moment of exhaustion on the ninth rep, the anxiety kicked its way in and you gasped. You couldn't lift the bar again. You sat up and started breathing rapidly, pushing back the urge to cry. You felt the muscles in your chest squeeze together, and then you got angry and lay back down and pushed through another set.

You can't believe one man is making you feel this lousy. One lousy jerk is causing you so much pain. You thought it would be much easier to get over this one. Why were you so foolish again? Why did you let yourself open up?

You open your eyes. You notice a cobweb hanging from the ceiling. Suddenly it makes you anxious. You want to get up and knock it down, but you can't move. You don't want to move. You wonder why you didn't go out of town this weekend. You knew you should have gone out of town. But you also knew you would have to work through this at some point. You can't keep running away. You can't keep taking the medicine. Or drinking. You've cleaned everything out of your sight that reminds you of him. You gave him back his cassette tapes, the T-shirt he slept in, his razor and toothbrush, even the photo he gave you for Valentine's Day.

But then yesterday he called and said he wanted to meet you for lunch. It had been exactly a week since you broke up for the third time. You thought he was going to suggest that you get back together, so you met him. You wanted to see him, see how he was doing. You missed him. Instead of saying he wanted to get back together, he spent the whole lunch alluding to the guy he was sleeping with now. It made you furious. You were wildly jealous. You wanted to know all the details, but you sat there silent, dumbfounded. You knew best not to ask about anything. And he knew that you knew and that it was driving you crazy. You think he was doing it out of spite, out of revenge, or even, perhaps, just out of meanness.

And then last night, you couldn't sleep at all. You spent the entire night angry, arguing with him in your mind. Liar, you called him. Jerk. Asshole. Cheater. Liar.

The cobweb is driving you crazy. You look away from it, turn on your side, and you notice a dust ball on the carpet. You have to get out of here, you think. You pull yourself up off the floor. You go directly to the back room where you keep your bike. You check the tires and then wheel it toward the door. You don't even waste time filling the canteen with water, looking for your radio, or getting your helmet. You are out the door as quickly as possible.

It is cloudy and gray outside. It is a warm summer afternoon, but the air feels heavy. You look up at the sky. It looks like there will be rain sometime today. You move so slowly you feel as though you are walking underwater. Every movement is lethargic and deliberate. You wonder if it is your stress or the humidity that makes you feel so sluggish. You push your bike. You open the gate. You walk out to the street. You look for traffic. First right. Then left. Then right again. You push the bike. You take tiny steps, placing one foot on the pedal and lifting and swinging your other leg over the bar. You glide down the street. Then you start pedaling. The motion feels thick, hard. You check the gears. It is in low. You pedal and glide, pedal and glide. In a few minutes, it will feel easier. You know. You know. You've done this before.

As you pedal, as you feel your body beginning to establish a rhythm, you begin to list the things that made you angry at him. Why you broke up. Why you were not right for each other. He was arrogant and obnoxious. He was too opinionated, and you didn't agree with his opinions. He thought Stanley Kubrick and David Lynch were always brilliant, but loved to tear whatever other movie or television show he saw into critical threads, criticizing the actor, the director, the producer, the editor, even the sound technician, pointing out every major flaw he observed. You couldn't stand the way he would refer to a woman as a "gal." He was self-absorbed, neurotic, psychotic. He loved to point out whenever you had a blemish on your face, when you nicked yourself shaving. He loved to correct you in public, whether it was your opinion or your pronunciation. Once he said you dressed like a blue-collar worker, and you knew he meant it as an insult.

So why, then, is he causing you so much pain? You pedal harder. You are approaching your first big hill. You notice everything is so green. Green grass, green trees, green fields. When you first met him everything was brown or gray. You only met him six months ago. Just as you were crashing from another boyfriend. Your first date was brunch. Your second was a movie. The third date you slept together. After that, you were together every night. Except when he went out of town. Except when he went out of town to see his lover.

You shake your head. You should have known better. How could you get involved with someone who was involved with somebody else? You knew right from the start there was another man. You were even cautious of your feelings for the longest time. But he said that they were having problems in their relationship. But then he also said he still loved him. He never said that to you. He never said he loved you to you. The first time you broke up with him, you said you were tired of being the third person in a relationship. You wanted something permanent. He didn't believe in permanent. But then he came back to you. Said he would work on it, but at the same time he went off to visit his lover. You feel he offered you a second chance and never came through with it. By the time he came back into town, you were both ready to break up again. You knew he had slept with his lover again, and he knew you knew he had done it. No words had to be said. But you still wanted him back, wanted to give a relationship with him a try. How could you let someone treat you like that? How could you get yourself so caught up in this man's confusion?

His confusion made you depressed. Your depression made him depressed. He was always restless, edgy. There was an unstable fire in his eyes. He was not good with words. He never paid you a compliment the whole time you saw each other. And there were comments he made that made you wonder if thinking and talking went together in his brain. One day he said you needed to lose some weight. Another day he said your baggy shirt made you look too thin. Many times he contradicted his own statements. If you pointed them out to him, he would say, "That was yesterday. Today is different."

You concentrate on the hill. It is the hardest one you will do, you know. You pedal, push, pull against the handlebars, keeping your balance. Over and over. You breathe through your mouth. You blow out. Inhale. Blow out. Inhale. Pedal. Push. At the top of the hill, you feel better. You are panting, breathing completely through your mouth. Your tongue feels dry. You smell honeysuckle and cut grass. You take the street on the right. You keep pedaling, pushing. You are still climbing, but the incline is easier now.

You see another biker approaching you. As the biker gets closer you notice it is a man. He is wearing a tank top. You can see the outline of the muscles of his arms. He is gliding downhill. You are pedaling, pushing. As you pass each other, you both nod and smile. You wonder if you will ever meet him. Thank God your ex-boyfriend never went biking with you, you think. Thank God you always kept this therapy to yourself. At least you don't have to remember biking with him. At least you don't have to imagine that. You feel the sweat underneath your arms and around the elastic band of your shorts. Already you feel better. Once you start the descent, it will be fun, relaxing. You know. You know. You remember. You've done this before. This is why you're doing it again.

The sun breaks through a cloud and hits your eyes. You squint, but the heat feels good. It makes you feel relaxed. You notice a rabbit hopping across the road. Suddenly you realize you miss him. You miss talking to him on the phone every day. You miss eating dinner with him. You miss touching him, kissing him, holding him. You miss him holding you. You miss the way everything became so chemical when you touched each other. Your chest aches remembering the way the tips of your fingers felt when they ran through the hair of his chest. You try to shake these thoughts from your mind, but you can't. You remember the way your hands fit around his waist, the smell of his skin, his underarms, his hair, his groin.

You defended him to your friends. They didn't like him. They said he was just after sex. And you had to defend him to yourself, in your own mind. There were times you felt, too, that he was only in it for the sex. You felt what he was doing was wrong, becoming involved with someone while he was involved with someone else. But you justified it because for the first time you could enter into something without any expectations. And you were lonely. And the sex was good. It made you feel good. You needed him as much as he needed you. You knew early on he was taken with you. The first time you met him you noticed his hands were trembling as he held a book in front of you to show you a passage. At first you wondered if anything was wrong with him physically, medically. Then you realized it was the way he carried his nerves, his stress. Later, the longer you dated, you noticed him become more confident. Then the arrogance appeared. Then you wished you had never met.

You stop pedaling. You begin to coast downhill. You feel a chill as the breeze hits your sweat. It feels good. You pass by the house you've always liked, the one you wish you could see inside. It is a log cabin with a lake in the back yard. Your head feels suddenly heavy. You cannot sleep at night because you miss him beside you. When you imagine him sleeping with someone else, you become angry, functionless. How can someone who knows how jealous you are tell you a story about how a man tried to pick him up on the train? How could he tell you that? The pain is back in your neck. You pedal, push, pedal, push, but you use up no energy—you are heading downhill. You breathe deeply. You concentrate on the wind, the motion, hitting your neck. You remember yesterday you, too, alluded to a date you had. And you knew it hurt him to hear it. You knew you hurt him. You are hurting and he is hurting and you are both waging a subconscious war with each other. You laugh out loud. Maybe this is the way you get over each other. Get over all this pain, pain, pain.

You swat at a gnat. You notice the leaves of the trees beginning to turn under. You wonder if it will rain before you get back to the house. You are not turning around. You are doing your loop, the one you always do when you need to unwind, clear your head.

You think about the things that make you feel better. You list them in your head: ice cream, biking, reading, movies, drawing, swimming, dancing, exercising, singing, jerking off. You knew all along your relationship with him was finite. It would not last. So why does it hurt? Maybe because you kept hoping it would work out. That he would change. That you would be the one to make him change. You think now that maybe he was too young. After all, he just turned thirty. He still has a lot to get out of his system. He hasn't been through your life and you are only four years older. But then you turn angry when you realize he never really wanted a relationship, did he? Certainly not the kind you wanted. He used you, you think. He used you for sex and now he's hurt you. Jerk, you think. Both of us. Both of them. You wonder where he is right now. You remember he went to Boston for the weekend to see a friend. Suddenly the pain is back. You feel anxious, restless. You want to be anywhere but where you are. You take deep breaths through your mouth. You think about calling up his answering machine and leaving an obscene or angry or obnoxious message. Jerk, you think. Liar.

You make a left turn and begin climbing another hill. You pass a man mowing his yard. Next door, rocks with painted faces on them are scattered across the lawn. You wonder if this makes the neighbor mowing mad. You pedal. Push. Pedal. Push. A heavy wind begins to blow the tops of the trees. You look up at the sky. The clouds are darker, thicker, more gray. The first time you broke up he asked you if you were mad or angry at him because he wanted to remain friends. "No," you said, "just disappointed." Now you can't even think of him as a friend. You don't even want him as a friend. Would a friend make you hurt so much? The next one will be better, you tell yourself. The next one. But where is the next one? Where will you meet him? *When* will you meet him?

You coast down the hill alongside a cornfield. You smell damp hay. A white convertible passes you from behind. You stare at the bald spot of the driver's head. He was never very romantic, you remember. You always wanted someone romantic. But then when you went to the concert or the movies or the theater, when the lights went out he would reach for and hold your hand. He gave up on you, you think. Not you on him. Every time. You wanted to fight to make it right. Make it work. Work things out. He gave up. Maybe you pushed him into a confrontation with himself, you think. Maybe you made him think. You made him make a decision. You needed a commitment. You needed to trust him. And so you lost. What you wanted was what he couldn't give you.

Okay, you think. Now you move on. Get over him. He was a jerk. Five years from now you are sure he will realize his mistake in letting you go. You are sure he realizes it now. But he's just a stubborn fool. More than you are. You know he is hurting. And a part of you hurts because you have hurt him.

But what about his lover? Or are they ex-lovers? That relationship was never, ever, clarified to you. How must his lover feel? How can he be so accepting of the situation? He knew about you. They're both jerks, you decide. Both of them. If he cheats on his lover, of course he's going to cheat on you. Isn't that the way it goes? You deserve better than that. You have your pride, your self-respect.

It couldn't go on. You know that. You couldn't live with the jealousy. It would have ended in violence, you are sure. You probably would have woken up one day and killed him. He deserved it. Jerk. Liar. But you still believe many of the things he said to you. He was attentive. He did want to live together. He wanted to meet your friends, your parents. He wanted to go with you to New York City and Atlanta and Washington and anywhere you wanted to go. But it was never meant to be. You can't forget that. You mustn't forget that.

You turn another corner. You are headed back to your house. You feel a raindrop splat you on the cheek. Then another on the top of your head. Then another on the shoulder, then the cheek, the nose, the brow, the cheek. Soon it is raining. You pedal. Push. Glide. Coast. By the time you see your house around the bend in the road, you are wet.

It shouldn't hurt, you tell yourself. You tell yourself this over and over. He was wrong. He was wrong. He wasn't the right one for you. You deserve better, you know. Liar. Jerk. Asshole. It will all pass. The rain will stop soon. So will the pain. You know. You know. You've been through this before. You know you deserve better. Pedal. Push. Pedal. Push. You're almost home. You know. You know.

What Does It Take?

You reach for the pillow. It is not there so you reach again and do not find it. You roll over, tuck your legs toward your stomach, stay in that position for three seconds, then reach out again for the pillow. It is not there. You struggle to keep your eyes shut. Your heart beats faster. The dream is gone. Lost. A nagging headache replaces it. You reach once more for the pillow and do not find it.

The pillow must have fallen to the floor. To reach it, to look for it on the floor, will take more effort. To find it will wake you. Completely wake you. You keep your eyes shut. You must hold them closed, fight off the urge to open them and look for the pillow. You roll over again, tuck your legs up. You try to sweep the sheet up into a ball beneath your head but your effort falls flat. Flat beneath the side of your head. You press your hand underneath your head, curl your fingers into a fist. Your head is slightly elevated but you feel the tension in your fist. You roll over and change positions in the bed, moving your head to where your feet were. This makes your heart beat faster. The headache nag a bit deeper. You fight to keep your eyes closed. You reach out again for the pillow, thinking it might be lost in this part of the bed. It is not there. It must have fallen on the floor while you were sleeping.

You concentrate on your breathing. Your eyes are still closed. You move the air slowly in and out of your body, thinking this will help you get rid of the growing headache and fall back asleep. You have not surrendered to the darkness of the room. You try to relax the spot in your head where the headache is centered. You breathe in and out. In and out. You grow more tense, tighter. The headache brightens. You feel blood rushing right to the spot of your headache. You reach out for the pillow and do not find it. You roll over onto your stomach, stay there for three seconds, then roll onto your side and tuck your legs up.

Your eyes are now open. The room is dark, full of your heartbeats. Slowly the edges of things come into view: a chair, a bookshelf by the window. You keep your breathing slow, your eyes feeling tired. Your throat is dry. Your tongue feels thick. You are thirsty. You should get up and drink a glass of water. Take an aspirin. You try to breathe the headache away, then the dryness in your mouth. You close your eyes, thinking you can still fall back asleep now that you have oriented yourself to your bedroom. Your apartment. Your home. You taste the dryness in your mouth. You feel it move across your teeth to your tongue and into the back of your throat.

You don't want to get up. You want to go back to sleep. If you sleep you won't have the headache when you get up. Your throat will not be dry. You will not be tired. Sleep will repair them, make everything all right. You tap your tongue at the corner of your lips to moisten them. Your throat fills with bitterness. Your stomach has awakened, has decided to communicate with your headache.

You roll over, place your fist beneath your head, and breathe slowly through your dry mouth. Your stomach rumbles. Is this from the Chinese food from dinner or the wine you had before you went to bed? You reach out again for the pillow thinking it might have just appeared like a miracle, like someone is watching out for you. Or over you. Of course it is not there. You are alone. You close your eyes. They open back up, as if controlled by a phantom puppeteer out for revenge. You breathe deeper. The headache widens. You are no longer sleepy though you are tired, exhausted, fighting off a headache, a dry mouth, and an upset stomach. You roll over and feel a cramp in your leg. What next? you think as you change the position of the cramping leg. It does not surprise you when it happens. Your stomach boils, sends gas down your intestines and makes it wait in your sphincter, ready to blow. You try to let it leak out, in a steady stream that will not wake you. But it wants to blow. You roll over into another position, hoping it will leak. The headache grows wider. Your throat is parched. Your stomach is making more gas. When the gas builds up more and more and you cannot hold it in any longer or let it leak out gently, you tighten your body, flex your buttocks, and let it blow.

o   o   o

You lie flat on your back. Your right hand is behind your head. You look up at the ceiling and take long breaths, trying not to smell your stench, wondering what it will take to fall back asleep. You begin by taking an inventory. You should not drink so much. You should not eat so poorly. You should get your teeth cleaned, buy some antacids. And eat more fiber. You should eat more fruit, more vegetables. Maybe stop meat, become a vegetarian. Stop taking so many herbs to help you sleep since they don't work. You should not bike so much so you don't get leg cramps in the middle of the night, join a gym to do different kind of exercises. You close your eyes, thinking that you have solved your problems by listing them. They blink themselves open. Your brain is not tired even though your body is exhausted. Why is this happening? Why can't you fall back asleep?

Did you forget to brush your teeth? Is that it? Are you being punished because you are thirty-five years old and did not brush your teeth before you went to bed? You did brush your teeth. Before the wine. Before the second glass of wine. No, you are being punished because you let your friend that you haven't seen in two weeks talk you into eating at that lousy Chinese restaurant. It's the soy sauce that is making you miserable. Or the green peppers that were soaked in soy sauce. Or the MSG that was in the soy sauce, even though the menu says it is never used. You blame it on the Chinese restaurant. Now you can fall back asleep. You have found the source of your problem.

You breathe in deeply again and wait for your stomach to

boil. It doesn't so you roll to your side, close your eyes, but you can sense the alarm clock beside you, emitting a bright red light. You open your eyes and read the time. 3:23. In bright red digital numbers. Why did you get this alarm clock with a bright, bright, bright red light? What possessed you to buy this devil?

You roll over to the other side of the bed, reach for the pillow. It is not there so you shove your hand beneath your head, tighten it into a fist. You see another light. More red digital numbers. The cable box on top of the TV is on. The numbers read 16. What were you watching when you went to sleep? When you started to go to sleep? You were drinking a glass of wine. The second glass or the third glass when you fell asleep? You were watching a tape, not the cable. You look down beneath the dark space that is the TV, where the VCR sits on the shelf. There is another red light. Smaller, tinier, but just as bright. You reach out on the bed, thinking you might find the remote control since you can't find the pillow. It is not there either. You look away from the VCR. Away from the cable box. You see another tiny red light in the distance. What the hell is that? you think. What the hell is that bright red light?

Your eyes search deeper into the darkness. Your headache grows stronger. It is the pest control device. Plugs into the electric outlet on the wall. A tiny red light keeps insects, roaches, and rodents out of your apartment. Tiny radio waves zap them away with a bright red light. It doesn't help. Yesterday you found a roach in the sink. Last week you chased a mouse into the wall. This pest control does a lousy job of controlling pests. It also stops you from falling back to sleep. Your pest control is becoming a pest. Why the hell did you spend your hard-earned money on that piece of no-good crap?

You roll over on your back again, look at the ceiling, a dark space without any bright red lights. You think about moving back to the city, into this apartment. Was this a mistake? To come back to a place you thought you had left behind? You had lived here ten years ago, a decade when your twenties became your thirties. You left because so many friends were dying. No, dead. They were dead. And you needed a change. You needed to have a breakdown. You needed to disassemble all the pieces of your psyche, clean and polish them, so you could come back stronger. That was it, wasn't it? You needed to leave so you could come back stronger.

You must not have done a very good job. Your head is now splitting. Whatever was clean is now certainly damaged. Or beyond repair. A tiny red light can make you crazy. Maybe you have a tumor. Or maybe you have become a full-blown mental case. That's it. That's why you can't sleep. You are now a full-blown deranged psychotic-neurotic and you will never be able to sleep soundly another minute of your adult life. You roll over to the corner of the bed, drop your hand to the floor. You move it back and forth, thinking it might touch the pillow if it fell on the floor. It is not there. You try to stay still to keep your head from pounding. It wasn't that bad in the country. All that grass and trees and flowers and bugs and dirt. It was just the wrong place at the wrong time. You were only gone two years from the city. What was it that you disliked so much about the country?

You try to change your position without moving your head. You flatten your neck against the bed, use your feet to twist the rest of your body into another place of the bed. It wasn't living in the country that made you crazy. It was guys who lived in the country who made you crazy. They were just as bad. They were just as messed up and confused and as non-committal as every other guy you ever met anywhere else in the world. They were just as bad as every guy you ever dated in this city for a decade before you left it.

o   o   o

You lie sideways on the mattress. Press your head against one edge, let your feet hang over the other side. Maybe this is the wrong approach. Maybe you should change your attitude, not focus on your shortcomings, or the shortcomings of any man you have ever met or dated or had sex with. Be positive. Positive energy will help you sleep. It will reinvigorate you, restore you, revitalize you, recharge you. You breathe in positive air. In and out. You are a positive being. Your headache is an asset. It makes you think, contemplate. You encourage your headache to grow, become one with you. You tell your headache to accept your thirst. Your desire for water is only a positive way of being in touch with your body. Your soul. The essence of life.

You roll over to your side. The red numbers of the alarm clock make you squint. You try to accept these numbers. 4:12. No, 4:13, as a positive source of energy. You cannot look at them. They are too bright. They are a bright, bright red. Their positive energy is blinding you, causing you to see spots in the darkness. Your headache is now overwhelming. There are dark spots in the dark night and they are making you stay awake. You close your eyes. What the hell are you trying to do? Your head feels like it is caught is a vise and now you see spots in front of your eyelids. You squeeze your eyes to make them disappear. The spots burst into an atom-bomb like mushroom of energy. Negative energy. Negative red energy. Your headache is exploding in front of your eyes.

You curl your body into a fetal position, stretch out an arm to see if you can touch the pillow, if it might have found its way to the center of the bed. It is not there and you let out a groan, a groan that makes the spots appear again before your eyes. Why did you have so much to drink? Why didn't you exercise some restraint? It was Dennis's fault. This all started with Dennis. Dennis was the reason why you drank so much tonight. He asked you what happened with Mark. Nothing happened with Mark. That's what you told him. You had three dates with Mark and then he went out of town on business and you never heard from him again.

"Did you call him when he got back?" Dennis asked.

"He never told me when he was coming back," you answered.

"Wasn't it just a business trip?"

"And a vacation."

"Why didn't you call him?" Dennis asked. "Why did you let this slide?"

You stretch out your body, the cramp in your leg is back. It throbs and grows. It talks to the headache. Your stomach boils. You roll over and curl your toes. The sheet is now twirled around your feet. You feel trapped, unable to move. You shift your leg and the twisted sheet comes with it. You move your leg again. The cramp stings, burns, has decided it wants to compete with the headache. You reach down and try to unravel the sheet from your feet. You can't figure out why it tightens around you. You tug. Tug some more. Finally, you let out a groan and lift your legs up off the bed and do a dance in the air, flutter kicking your feet until the sheet is free. And so are your feet.

Now the headache is greater than the cramp. It makes your toes ache. Your breathing is hard. Your heart is beating faster. How many dates are you supposed to have before a guy will sleep with you? Mark didn't even want to kiss you. It was the right friend fixing you up with the wrong guy. There was no chemistry. No attraction, one way or another. Why did you even bother to go out the second or third time? Why didn't you just both admit defeat? You blame it on Dennis. It was all Dennis's fault. Why do friends feel the need to fix you up with lousy blind dates?

o   o   o

You try another position. You lie on your side, stretch out your arm, rest your head on your shoulder. You breathe through your mouth. You touch your tongue to the roof of your mouth. You draw the moisture out of your throat. Your stomach rumbles. The red numbers are right in front of your eyes. Bright, bright red. 4:29. You close your eyes. Imagine the red numbers getting higher, the night progressing, the day arriving. 4:45. 5:15. 6:01. Daylight breaking through. Now it's time to get up. You open your eyes and it is still dark. You decide to try another approach.

If you imagine that you are sleeping maybe you will fall back asleep. You can fool your mind. You imagine yourself lying in bed. Then, you imagine you are on the ceiling, looking down at your body, sleeping, restoring itself, relaxing. At peace. You look at yourself shift in the bed. Then shift again. Something is wrong. Something is terribly wrong. It is your head. Your head is reminding you that it is aching. You tighten your shoulder, tense the muscle, then let it relax. You imagine the blood flowing through your body evenly, without blockage or discomfort, the veins and arteries widening for a smooth flow of pumping blood. Is this all your fault? Are you single and miserable because you are too demanding? Ray had a lover already when you met him. Arnie was still mourning the loss of his partner. Ross was just in it for the sex. Jack wouldn't leave his wife and kids. Bryan wanted you to be someone you were not. Is that it? Is that why you can't find a guy and if you do you can't keep him? Is it all your fault and none of his? Is something wrong with you?

Of course there is something wrong with you. Your head is splitting. Your throat is dry. Your life is so miserable you cannot fall asleep. You turn over, stretch your legs out. Your back aches. The bed is lumpy. You have found a crater in your mattress and you are now sinking into it. You are sinking so deep into your mattress that your body contorts itself as it is sucked into the hole of your lumpy piece of crap that you got at a not-so bargain price. You struggle to breathe. You toss, turn, find a way out of the hole and onto another part of this lumpy thing that is impersonating a mattress. In the distance you see the bright red light of the pest control device. You flip over onto your back, look at the ceiling where there are no red lights. You will try one more approach. One more way to get your mind to relax. You will count your blessings.

You fold your fingers together. Form a church, like you did when you were a boy, point two fingers to create a steeple. You close your eyes. You become one with the darkness. Thank you, God, for letting me have a place to live, even though I have to work three jobs and seventeen hour days seven days a week to afford it. Thank you, God, for making me attractive enough to make another guy interested enough in having sex with me for twenty or so minutes even though he has no intention of wanting a conversation or ever hear the sound of my voice. Thank you, God, for giving me friends who want to see me miserably fail on blind dates. And thank you, God, for my health, even though I pray to you now to release me from my discomfort. Please, God, take my headache away from me and give it to one of my blind dates. Or give it to the guy I was tricking with two days ago that I met coming out of the subway stop. Give it to my landlord for overcharging me. Give it to the insects and roaches and rodents who hide in my walls and drains and kitchen cabinets.

You are so still you can feel the blood pumping into your skull. Your headache is saying hello to each and every blood cell. You break the church up, run a hand through your hair, press a palm against your forehead, thinking the pressure might draw your headache out of your body. No such luck. You trail your fingertips along your forehead, across the temple and down to your cheek. You hear nothing but the sound of your dry skin. It is so loud your eyes pop open. Your dry skin reminds you of your dry mouth. You want a drink of water and an aspirin but you refuse to get out of bed. You refuse to admit that you are defeated and cannot fall back asleep because there is still a chance that it could happen. You roll over onto your side, look at the bright red digital numbers. 4:32. Hell, you think. I have been sent to hell.

o   o   o

You turn over, lie on your stomach. Press your head into the mattress. You feel the center of your headache shift, wobble. You breathe in the warm, damp air you just exhaled. You are recycling your moisture, refueling your cells. You breathe out warm air. You breathe in moist air. Your headache reminds you it is still here, begging for attention. You pretend to ignore it, breathing in and out. You shift your attention to your cramping leg, your upset stomach. You will not give your headache its due. You continue to breathe. In this position you feel your body bearing down against your stomach. Your stomach drops against the mattress, sags into the crater of the bed. You use your back to pull it up and the ache widens along your waist. This makes you breathe harder, faster. Suddenly you realize you are aroused, your cock is growing larger, drawing in the blood because it is now the lowest part of your body, the thing that gravity is pulling back to earth. You press your groin into the mattress, rub back and forth. The hardening cock is releasing you from the headache.

You continue to rub your groin back and forth. Tiny little bursts of pleasure work their way up your body to your brain. Your stomach stops rumbling. Your mouth fills with saliva. The leg cramp is gone. You push a hand beneath your body and grab your cock. The heat of it fills your hand. You tighten your grip, release it, tighten it again. You are astonished by the relief. The pleasure makes you continue.

You roll over and the air above you is cool and moist. You continue to hold your cock, giving it encouraging little nudges. Your eyes are closed. You are exhausted and tired and sleepy but full of pleasure. The headache has been frightened away. You use your hand to keep yourself aroused. Why didn't you do this before if this is what you needed? Why didn't you think about this sooner?

Your mind fills with images. You sort through them, pick out your favorites. The guy in the deli three days ago. The actor in the cereal commercial. The man on the fourth floor of the building where you temp. You isolate a face. A forearm. A mustache. You hold each one in front of you, stroking. You pull and grasp and clutch and grip. Your body lightens. You feel as if you are floating. You are nothing but sensation.

Your headache breaks forth just as you ejaculate. It surfaces, pesters the center of the skull, frightens the guys away. You lie on your back with your hand wet and sticky. You fight off the urge to move, not wanting to encourage the headache to shift. As you breathe your mouth becomes dry. Your stomach rumbles to remind you that it is still around and filling up with gas. You feel yourself dripping into the hair of your groin. You flatten your palm against your stomach, hoping your mess will disappear, evaporate into the darkness. You don't want to move. You don't want to give up your final sensations of pleasure. You don't want to get out of bed. You want to go back to sleep.

A sound from the street makes you roll over to face the window. Glass breaking, a bottle being thrown against a brick wall. You hear a truck gunning down the street toward the tunnel. Through the window the dark blue sky is beginning to lighten. You watch the sun do its work. You breathe slowly in and out as dark becomes gray becomes pale becomes ash becomes light. It happens quickly. The room brightens, more details come into place: the clothes you left on the chair. The spines of books on the shelves. The digital numbers disappear. The red lights are no longer bright. Your headache lessens. Your eyes become heavy, tired. Your body sinks against the bed, the muscles relax. You cannot move because you are exhausted. You close your eyes just as the sun is streaking into your room. You fall asleep minutes before the alarm tries to wake you. You roll over, hit the devil, and fall back asleep. Sleep is your agenda for the day. That's all you want to do.

What You Know of Him

Something about him makes you look again. Your glance shifts even though Dennis is talking to you. You are leaning against the side of the wall, in the back of the room. The room is full of conversations. The meeting has not yet started.

Dennis is talking about politics—the upcoming primary, the demonstration in midtown. His eyes follow yours to the man who has caught your attention. The man is out of place because of his suit. Gray, pinstripe. White shirt, conservative tie. The man is carrying a briefcase. He is walking through the room toward an empty seat, around a group of men in white T-shirts, jeans, heavy black boots.

It is not the suit that you noticed. The suit caught your attention. But the face is what made you look again. It is a face you have not seen in a long time. It is clean shaven. No mustache. No goatee. Out of place in this room of facial hair. The balding scalp is natural, not shaved, not hidden by a backwards baseball cap. The face, the man, the suit—even the briefcase—do not look any older than when you last saw them so many years ago. You feel like the one who has aged, instead.

The man stops at an empty seat, places his briefcase on the floor. He stands, stretches his back, looks out at the room, in your direction. He looks right through you. He shows no indication that he knows you, has even seen you. You think about how your appearance has changed since you last saw him. The gym has made you tougher. The goatee makes you look older. Time has erased your boyish edge.

The man continues to look around the room, as if he is looking for someone special. A particular person. His eyes look deeper now, closer. Into groups, conversations. You wonder who he is missing. Who he has missed. When he looks at you again, he takes you in. You smile and nod at him. He smiles back at you, nods. You hope he remembers you, then feel foolish if he doesn't. Or does. Your goatee makes you feel silly, insecure. Your short hair makes you feel bare, vulnerable. You feel like an impostor who has been suddenly uncovered. You don't belong here any more than he does. You are not the man you thought you were.

The man shifts his eyes to Dennis, takes Dennis in. The goatee, the shaved head, the double earrings in the left ear. The white T-shirt, black jeans, black boots. You wonder if he thinks that Dennis is your boyfriend, if he thinks that you are a couple. Settled for a lover after all, did you? you can hear him thinking. And this is what finally worked for you: facial hair and a gym membership.

Dennis continues talking about politics. The man in the suit is of no interest to him. You continue to pretend you are listening to Dennis instead of watching the man look around the rest of the room. His gaze does not slow. Only pauses here and there. He continues his search. You wonder who he hopes to find. And if he expects to find him here tonight.

You know he is living downtown again. On Grove Street. He either sold or subleases the apartment on East 55th Street. You know this because you looked him up in the phone book last month or maybe the month before. After a blind date. With another man. Every time you have a bad blind date with a guy, where even sex is not a possibility, you return home and look up the man in the phone book. *What if?* you think. *What if it had worked out? What if you had not been so needy? Confrontational? Young? Inexperienced?*

Sometimes you dial his number, listen to see if his answering machine picks up. You only call when you think he will not be around. When you will not interrupt anything. Only get the recorded voice. You usually call from work so if he happens to be home you can say, "Sorry, wrong number," without him knowing it was you calling to hear his voice. He has never answered when you call. You have not spoken to him in ten years. Or is it eleven? You have only heard his voice occasionally, when you need to hear it, on the answering machine. Sometimes when you get a hang-up on your answering machine you think that it was him, checking in on you, too, wondering what it would have been like if things had worked out.

You wonder why it has taken you so long to run into each other again. The city is not that big, really. There are not that many guys here. Not any more. Not with so many leaving for one reason or another. Moving away. Dying. Changing jobs. Changing lovers. It turned out to be a bigger life than the small world you thought it was. You think about all the guys who have come and gone since he did not work out. This thought makes you dizzy. Anxious. As if there is something more wrong with you and less wrong with him. You look at Dennis and then look away again, out into the room. You notice the man is looking in your direction. You see his stare has changed, turned inward. You think he is thinking about you: You think he is wondering, remembering, dismissing your past.

o   o   o

After the meeting starts you stay in the back of the room, leaning against the wall. Dennis stands next to you while the announcements are being made. There are announcements and more announcements. Someone interrupts the announcements to remark on the order of the announcements. Someone else checks the rules of procedure, a discussion is briefly raised and squashed, and the announcements continue. Dennis shifts and grows uneasy when another announcement interrupts the order of announcements; he is ready to talk. He is part of tonight's agenda. He has something to say. You look at the speaker in the center of the room and try not to notice the naturally balding head of the man wearing a suit who is in the corner of your vision. It occurs to you that you will not talk to him at all tonight. Your opportunity of speaking with him, of catching up with his life, was lost once the meeting started. These meetings last hours and hours. You can seldom stay to the end anymore. Everyone has an agenda, something to say. All this anger has lost its fascination for you. You are only here because Dennis asked for your support, though you doubt Dennis will even remember you are here once he begins talking, once his own agenda becomes the agenda of the meeting.

Dennis is short and muscular. He likes to display his body in tight clothes. In the summer he only wears tank tops. You think that this is because he is positive and wants to appear invulnerable and full of health. He has known his sero-status for seven years, since he took the blood test. He is certain he has been positive for almost fourteen years because he believes his thirteenth boyfriend infected him. His thirteenth boyfriend, Roger, had lymphoma and has been dead for eight years. Roger's death was the first great blow in Dennis's life. It turned Dennis into a relentless critic. Dennis plans on complaining when he speaks tonight. There is a local doctor who has annoyed him and he plans to protest his treatment.

If Dennis knew the whole story of the man in the suit he would tell you you are better off without him. First he would roll his eyes, then he would tell you you are better off. Next he would say something like, "You can do better than that." Then he would drop the subject of you and turn the subject back to himself. You first met Dennis at a support group for co-dependents eight years ago when a blind date said you had issues you needed to deal with. At that meeting, Dennis complained for close to twenty minutes about his therapist because he was now dating Dennis's ex-boyfriend. Dennis ranted and raved, went on and on about the fact that those two guys were mismatched and what could they possibly see in each other that they didn't see in him. You became friends when you interrupted his monologue and said, softly, almost under your breath, "Well, at least they have you to talk about."

98

You first met the balding man in the suit at a bar four blocks from where this meeting is being held. Eleven years ago. He had a bit more hair then, but not much more. He was standing by a juke box, drinking a beer in a bottle. It was summer, late summer, almost fall because he was not wearing shorts. You were twenty-six. He was almost forty. You thought he was the most handsome thing you had seen that day. You wanted him to know you. You wanted him to be a part of your life. You went back to his apartment and had sex. He gave you his number and said he wanted to see you again.

You shift the way you are standing to look at the back of his neck. Eleven years is a long time not to see someone. What if he doesn't remember you? What if you were like someone he met at the baths, or in a backroom? A nameless, physical sensation? What if he has forgotten the details you remember? He was an insurance claims adjuster. Or a claims processor. Or an insurance analyst. Something like that. On your second date you went to the movies. Or was it a play? Your third or fourth date you took him out for a birthday dinner; you ate a place where the waiters were too handsome. Or too young. Together, you even entertained another couple: you cooked duck for two dark-haired guys who looked like brothers. The thought of that evening makes you depressed, uneasy. While you were helping him wash dishes you knew it was not going to work out. You had nothing to talk about except whether the dishes were clean or still greasy. You were waiting to have sex. And so was he.

o   o   o

When the speakers change and someone questions the procedure of choosing the next speaker, you walk to the side of the room and pick up copies of articles which have been left on the table. There is an article on a needle exchange program and an article on the ineffectiveness of the President. You fold them in half and walk out of the meeting and into the lobby of the building. You sit on the steps and wish you still smoked so you could kill some time, though you are glad you no longer dependent on that habit. You look at the articles and decide to read them later, zipping them up into your backpack.

You wonder what you would say to him if he were to walk out into the lobby right now, looking for you while you are looking in your backpack. After all these years, it would probably go like this:

"How are you?" you would ask him.

"I am fine," he would answer. "How are you?"

"I am fine, too," you would say.

You can't tread water in a shallow pond, you think. You never had the kind of adventure with him that you have had with Dennis. With Dennis you have gone to the beach, to pride parades, to a demonstration in Washington. On Christmas Eve, Dennis takes his closest friends to see the worst movie of the year. Last summer, he threw a pool party in his tiny Hell's Kitchen apartment. The invitation suggested "Cock Tails" and "Swim Attire." When the postcard showed up in your mailbox you knew this was Dennis being narcissistic: He could care less what anyone else was drinking as long as he had a good excuse to show off his body.

You decide it is better that you did not talk to the man, did not approach him even if it was just to hear the sound of his voice again. When you dated him there was nothing to talk to him about. You talked about nothing because you were both waiting to have sex. The third and fourth dates you tried to do other things so it would not look like you were so eager to hop into bed again.

You remember the first night at his apartment. It was a fourth-floor walk-up. There was a Persian rug that snagged the door. In the bedroom, he kept on his T-shirt because he said he had a bad rash. It didn't matter to you because he had a big dick which he was eager to show you. Thick as a beer can, as the saying goes. You can see Dennis smirking if you told him that. "No wonder you kept coming back," he would accuse you. "Because you're as shallow as he is."

Once in a while you still think about him. You remember him in bed: on top of you, against you, around you, inside you. In your recollection he brings you comfort. Safety. Stability. Desire. Even though it was only sex. Protection was not even a thought when you dated him. Nobody used a condom because nobody was worried then. You wonder what Dennis would make of this. What would the man make of this today? What would he say if you told him you had slept together more than a thousand times in your mind and every time you did it it was still unsafe sex?

o   o   o

Back in the meeting a thin, blond-haired lesbian is reporting on a subcommittee. She looks like a tough little boy, the kind who would be your best friend and always get you into trouble. When she finishes Dennis takes the floor and begins to explain his complaint. The room is quiet. There are a few nods and a tapping of feet in agreement. Someone in the corner is taking notes. When he finishes he asks for questions and there is a rush of hands toward the ceiling.

You look at where the man is seated to see if he has a question, too. He is no longer in the chair. A chunky woman with a braided pony tail has taken his place. You look at the table to see if he is there. He is not. You scan the back walls. The side walls. The front table. He is not there, either.

You walk out into the lobby. There is no sight of him so you return to the meeting feeling desperate, defeated, as if you are being punished for being a shallow man. In the front of the room Dennis is answering another question. His face his red. The veins in his neck are big. You wonder if these meetings are dangerous for him. A strain on his heart. If it could make him lose a few T-cells he cannot afford to lose.

When he motions for another question, you realize the man is standing next to you. You don't know what to do. You stare straight ahead until it seems like staring straight ahead is the wrong thing to do. You relax your shoulders. You turn toward him. He reaches out his hand and you instinctively reach out yours to greet him. You shake hands. Your eyes meet. Then it is over and you are both looking at Dennis's big red face again.

o   o   o

"Do you think I did okay?" Dennis asks you when the meeting is over. "Do you think they understood what it felt like?"

It is late and you are tired, but you attend to Dennis's neuroses because that is what you are here to do. "I think it was important that you talked about that," you say. "No one else is speaking up about it."

Dennis only lets the sentiment register for a second. He turns and asks another person the same question, a young guy with a goatee wearing a tight white T-shirt who reminds you of a younger version of Dennis. You walk to the other side of the room to retrieve your backpack. When you lift it off the floor you wonder what could possibly make it feel so heavy. Then the thought occurs to you that maybe the man in the suit did not recognize you. Maybe he didn't remember you at all. You were the one who smiled at him before the meeting. You were the one who made the first move, turned to him first. He was just standing there, pretending you did not exist.

He did not stay much longer after the handshake. He seemed embarrassed, as if he had forgotten to say what he intended to say. He left you there feeling the pressure of his hand and the soft whisper of his "hi." No, that was you, that wasn't him who said "hi;" it was you. You, you, you said hello. He said nothing.

You decide to tell Dennis that you are leaving but see that he has already left without you. He is no longer in the room. He is not in the lobby. Outside, in the night, you see his shadow within a group of men. You think about just leaving, talking to him tomorrow on the phone. You lift your backpack around your shoulder and set out on your path around the men. As you walk by the group you see that the man in the suit is standing next to Dennis. He is talking to Dennis. Beside him is a blond-haired guy with a mustache: tall, thin, and also wearing a tie. He was not at the meeting. You are certain of that. You would have noticed another man wearing a tie, especially one who was friendly with the one wearing the suit.

Dennis stops you as you walk by, says he will go uptown with you. He introduces you to the group of men. "Bill," "John," "Dennis," "Pete" are the names that you make out. The blond guy in the necktie has a strong enough grip to make you feel threatened. You know instinctively that the blond guy has something to do with the man in the suit. You have no doubt. Dennis continues talking about his doctor's visit until the blond man in the neck tie says that they must go. As they walk away from you, you notice the man in the suit drape his arm around the blond-haired man with a neck tie, the arm which is not carrying his briefcase. They walk closer together into the night. This is something the man in the suit carrying the briefcase would never have done eleven years ago. Of that you are certain.

o o o

On the subway Dennis is quiet without an audience. His body looks smaller than it really is. The train rattles and shakes and you feel the extra pounds of your stomach. You think you need to do more sit-ups. You look at your reflection in the window and think you would not even recognize yourself if you met yourself eleven years ago. You have changed that much.

On the ride, staring at your older self, you remember the reason why you broke up with him. He gave you crabs. Or was it the clap? The fourth or fifth time you were together you did it on the floor by the door. You had rug burns on your elbows. A few days later you had a drip. There was a phone conversation with him where you suggested that he get tested. And another phone conversation where he said you didn't get anything from him. You called him a few times to apologize, to tell him that it was your all fault and none of his, that you had been out to the baths with a friend a few days before and, well, things had happened and you didn't want to tell him what they were.

But he was never home when you called. So you kept calling him. And calling. And then you just needed to hear his voice. So you continued to call.

What Comes Around

You are thirty-seven and eleven-twelfths. Or fifteen-sixteenths. It is the eve of your thirty-eighth birthday. You look into the mirror and try to decide who you are. You are not handsome, or so you think. You are not ugly, either, you decide. In this city, this city of drop-dead gorgeous actors and models, you are somewhere in between. Somewhere in between is what you are. You are an almost thirty-eight year-old gay man who is somewhere in between drop-dead gorgeous and troll-like ugly.

You turn and study your profile in the mirror. It is not a strong profile. But it is not weak one, either. Your hairline has receded but you are not bald. You do not have a bald spot but you no longer have a full head of teenaged hair. You no longer have beautiful brown bangs. You no longer have to push your long brown hair out of your eyes. You look at yourself again in the mirror, this time deeper at the hairline. You do not have any gray hair, either. You are a guy approaching forty without any graying hair.

You weakest spot is your chin, you decide. It is all about your chin, you think when you study your profile again. You have never liked your chin from this angle. Your chin is up but it is not defying gravity. You notice too much skin on your neck. You turn and study your chin from the other side. You decide you don't like that angle either. You face the mirror. You like this position best. The dimple in your chin is now faint. But prominent. You decide this is who you are. You are not a right or a left profile kind of person. You are a straight-forward kind of guy. The kind of guy with a faint but prominent dimple in his chin who hopes someone doesn't notice his developing turkey neck.

You are not in the habit of dwelling on your looks. Not when you have a boyfriend. Or a date. When you have a boyfriend or a date you do not study your looks so much. When you have a boyfriend or a date you are outwardly focused, not inwardly obsessed. But since it is the eve of your birthday and you have neither a boyfriend nor a date everything is out of sync. Forty is looming. You are approaching a time zone of trauma. Everything loses perspective when you realize forty looms closer. You wonder if you are capable of still finding a boyfriend or a date in a city where there are so many drop-dead gorgeous actors and models as your competition, and most of whom are now younger than you are.

It is the morning of the eve of your thirty-eighth birthday and you have no plans tonight. Dennis is busy with a new boyfriend. Jack is never available. You have plans tomorrow night with Peter but no plans tonight. You could rent a movie tonight, but you are too restless. You want to get out of the your apartment. Your planets are all in the place where they are supposed to be and you do not want to be in the house tonight. You are supposed to be at your zenith. You are not forty but you are not twenty, either. You are not as attractive as you were ten years ago but you should be ten years smarter. You should use your experience to keep yourself entertained. You should know what you want to do tonight.

So what should you do? You could call a phone line, hook up with someone for sex, but you did that earlier in the week and it would feel like a desperate thing to do tonight. You do not want to be desperate. Or act desperate. You could jerk off and then decide to call the phone line, that way you wouldn't have to get off because you already did. The necessity of it would be gone and you could simply have a good time getting someone else off. You decide that is an outwardly focused idea and not something to do when you are inwardly obsessed. You decide that you should do something other than look for sex. So what should you do? Ten-plus years' worth of wisdom tells you you should go out and look for sex.

You decide you will go to a bar. You stomach churns at the thought. Your stomach always churns and bubbles when you think about going to a bar. It is an ingrained habit. It's as if your stomach knows you will drink too much and then try to soak it all in with a quick stuffing of donuts or pizza before you go to sleep to prevent a hangover the next morning. You decide you will go out to a bar and have only one drink. Your stomach calms down but it is not convinced. One drink barely sets you at ease in a bar but your stomach rumbles with appreciation.

You rinse your face at the sink, dry it with a towel, pull your underwear off, and sit on the toilet. You pick a magazine off the floor that you picked up at a bar the last time you were out, four days ago. This magazine comes out every week. Every week there is another handsome young man on the cover, a drop-dead gorgeous model or actor getting paid for what he does best—look like a drop-dead gorgeous cover boy. If he is not handsome then he is beautiful or sexy. Sometimes the cover features a porn star. If he is not beautiful or sexy or a porn star then he has a great set of abs. Or arms. Or chest. Or something else. You are not something else or any of the above. You are almost thirty-eight years old and you are spending your morning of the eve of your last day as thirty-seven on the toilet reading a magazine you picked up in a gay bar four days ago.

You study the magazine like it was a text book. You read the advertisements. There is a party for a drag queen which you will not go to because you are not a pretty faux-blond boy or a beautiful faux woman. There is another party on a boat which you will not go to because it will make you seasick. There is a party for the launch of a new CD and another one for the launch of a new movie. You live in a city of parties that you never go to. You are not a pretty party boy. Faux-blond or otherwise.

In fact, you are not good at parties. You have never been good at parties. The one you threw in seventh grade stank. (No one made out.) The one in high school was a bomb. (Everyone made out except you.) In college you went to parties where you didn't fit in. (You didn't want to make out with a girl.) Two decades later in the city you can no longer make small talk at a party. You are not a small talk kind of guy.

You flip through the pages of the magazine till you reach the personal ads at the back. You begin to read the small type. It is so small it makes your eyes squint. This gives you a bit of a headache but you continue reading this way. You think you might find another no-small-talk kind of guy. You hope there is another no-small-talk kind of guy looking to meet the same.

What you find is what you are not. You are never the same as the guys who are looking. This happens every time you read the personals. Every time you discover you are not what someone else is searching for. You are not an in-shape Latino. You are not an Italian bubble butt bottom. You are not a hot muscle uncut horse-hung top. There is an Hispanic guy into poppers looking to hook up with other brothers. (Not you.) Another guy is looking for a slender Asian with big nipples. (No, not you, either.) A master wants to give orders to someone into SM, BD, WS, CBT, FF, TT and any kind of kink. (No, sorry, not you, either.) You wonder what kind of kink any-kind-of-kink is if the master has already listed all of the other stuff. Enemas, you decide. The master didn't list enemas, did he? You decide the kind of kink this guy is looking for is enemas and you are not the one to give it to him.

You continue reading and squinting. At least you are working out your facial muscles, you think. At least this activity is burning up some calories even though it is creating a big sense of depression and an almost-headache. You are not nine-and-a-half or more. You are not a slave who can shoot a big load. You do not want to be humiliated by someone smoking a cigar. When you reach the end of the page you realize that what you want is not in this magazine. You want a three-dimensional no-small-talk kind of guy who wants to meet another one, or at least one with a faint but prominent dimple in his chin.

You realize you have spent too much time reading this magazine. You realize that this could make you seem shallow to a potential boyfriend, studying personal ads as if they were formulas that could cure the epidemic. You wipe and flush even though there was no action back there. Your toilet is simply a great place to catch up on reading the magazines you pick up in a gay bar. You pull up your underwear. You turn on the water at the sink, rinse your face again, open the cabinet, and pull out the shaving crème.

You lather up your face. You dip the razor in the running water. You are about to shave away the last beard of your thirty-seventh year. It makes you pause in front of the mirror and study yourself again. You think about growing back your goatee. Your goatee was multi-colored. Brown around your lips, blond at the corners, black at your chin. It was not a good goatee but it was good for sex. You got plenty of cruises and plenty of sex when you had a goatee. Guys found you more approachable with a goatee. They talked to you in a bar. They bought you drinks. They took you back to their apartments. But you never saw the same guy twice. A goatee did not help you find yourself a boyfriend. A goatee was no help to you. And it hid your faint but prominent dimple. You were not a goatee sort of guy. What you wanted was not another guy with a goatee. What you wanted was a guy who would call you back.

You look into the mirror and think about being someone different. Someone not just clean shaven with a weak, dimpled chin and a receding hairline. If you were someone different you wouldn't be a no-small-talk kind of guy without a goatee and with nothing to do on the eve of his thirty-eighth birthday.

You look first at your hair. You imagine yourself with a different haircut. You could cut it shorter or shave it all off. You are not the short-short-hair type of guy. You also do not have the proper shape of a head to shave it all off. You try to imagine yourself with a bald scalp but you are haunted by a vision of when you tried to be faux-blond. Your one attempt to be a faux-blond left you looking like a copper shag carpet—your hair became a strange, reddish color and broke into a million brittle split ends. You did not even make a good faux-blond. You were miserable for days, weeks, months, before it all disappeared. You could not bring yourself to cut your hair short even when it was riddled with a million brittle split ends. You could certainly not shave it all off. You were stuck with wearing caps wherever you went. You avoided swimming in pools, not wanting your copper-colored shag carpet to turn green. Your hair is fine, you decide. You will keep it the way it is. Nice and brown and natural.

You think next about getting your ear pierced. If you had a pierced ear then maybe you would not seem so uptight. You try to imagine what you ear would look like pierced and decide it would not be a good look for you. A stud would look out of place on your ear. Like a mole or a freckle. You are not a hoop-earring sort of guy, either, though you think it might be fun to wear something that dangled. You think again about your lost hairline, the time many, many, many years ago when you grew your hair so long that it whooshed when you turned your head. This is what comes around year after year after year. Your hair changes without your help, whether you want to be bald, faux-blond, or otherwise.

This thought makes you depressed so you look at your ears again. You have good ears but not a good pierced-ear look. You think one pierced ear would set you off-balance. You are all about balance because you are a Libra. You are a thirty-seven year-old gay man watching himself turn thirty-eight before his eyes.

You look down at your chest. You think about piercing your nipple. Or nipples since you would have to have a balance there, too. This makes you laugh. You are not a nipple pierced kind of guy either. You think briefly about a tattoo. A chain link line around a non-existent bicep. You lift your arm and flex your non-existent bicep. No matter how much you pump iron your muscles do not seem to grow into muscles. The only thing that really grows is your whole body. Every year you grow a little bit older. That is what grows. This is what changes. Your body becomes heavier. It becomes harder and harder to fight gravity.

You step away from the sink and look at yourself in the full length mirror on the back of the door. You try not to laugh at yourself, even though you look like an undressed Santa Claus with your beard of shaving crème. You pull in your stomach, lift up your buttocks. Maybe you should pierce your navel, you think. That is the center of you, your middle point. This makes you laugh harder and you lose your posture. Then this makes you upset. And more depressed. You look at your stomach and decide that your pierced navel might make someone else sick. Your navel is not flat because your stomach is not flat. No matter how hard you exercise you cannot get your stomach to be flat. You do not have any abs. You have never seen your abs. You will never see your abs. You are almost thirty-eight years old and your potential set of abs are history. All you can hope for is that your waist size will never again be a number larger than your age.

You return to the mirror in front of the sink again. You start to shave. You think again about all the things you are not in this city of drop-dead gorgeous actors and models and porn stars. You could be worse off, you think. You could not be someone stuck somewhere in the middle but further down the rung. You could be someone trying to impersonate a faux-blond, you think. You could be an aging self-absorbed wanna-be faux-blond guy and someone a lot dumber than you are. You shave some more, decide that what you are is lucky you are not a wanna-be faux-blond and self-absorbed. Well, at least not a wanna-be faux-blond, you correct yourself. You would not be happy if you still wanted to be blond.

What You Fear

Your first mistake was to start cooking before you had coffee. Your second was to add too much milk to the batter. You add more flour to the mix and let it sit for a moment instead of stirring. You find a coffee cup in the cupboard, the jar of instant in the refrigerator. You shake out the powder, pour the boiling water into the cup, and the let the steam rise into your face. The smell makes you hungry so you swirl the batter for a few stirs, dip your finger in and take a taste. You add milk to the cup and more milk to the batter because it is now too thick. You sip and stir, sip and stir, finally shaking off your sleepiness.

When your brain clears you realize you forgot to use the new wooden spoon Wade showed you the night before. You find it in the drawer, dip it into the batter, use it to smash a few lumps of flour against the side of the bowl. Since you've been dating Wade, more than a year now, he has added new items to his kitchen for you to use while you cook—the stainless steel mixing bowl, the spice rack, the pot holder, and now the new wooden spoon. The waffle maker was your Christmas gift to him, your way of showing you could pamper him. Wade says he likes being pampered. He says he likes to wake up to a big breakfast with you on Sunday mornings. And you like cooking while he putters around the bathroom. It makes you forget about things back at your own apartment, the floor that is never cleaned, the shelves of books that are never dusted, the messages on your answering machine about the bills that you are late paying. In his kitchen you are in control of your life, your anxieties, your relationship.

Your logic is if things work out in here then they will work out in other places, that what goes right in one place will spread joy and happiness and contentment into others. But the truth of the matter is that the cooking also keeps you from looking for clues to Wade's dissatisfaction with your relationship or searching for the things he might be hiding from you, things he thinks you do not want to know but, of course, you really do want to know (but without him knowing that you know them).

When you hear Wade turn the water on in the bathroom you oil the plates of the griddle. You have practiced your recipe for months. You've experimented with adding cinnamon and nutmeg and ginger and maple syrup directly into the batter. You've tried cooking the waffles with sunflower oil, corn oil, and extra virgin olive oil (which usually turns out to be the best). Even the timing has been carefully practiced. By the time Wade is out of the shower, you have the table set, the glasses filled with juice, and the last set of waffles are browning on the griddle.

He gives you a funny look when he arrives in the kitchen and sits at the table. You look swiftly around the table, wonder what is wrong, what you have forgotten.

"Your hair," he says. "It's standing up like a wave."

Your third mistake was not combing your hair so that you look like a grown-up eating breakfast with another adult. Your fourth mistake was something you have no control over. You come from a long line of bad cooks. Your grandmother never passed along any recipes. You mother serves everything unintentionally blackened. Your sister makes potato salad that resembles soup. Even your niece is in on the family secret. She makes waffles worse than you. Your fifth mistake of the morning was looking into the garbage before you tossed the soggy waffles into the pail. You must not have seen the yellow post-it while you were cooking. You lift it out of the pail, shake off the egg shells and flour. The name and numbers written on it are still legible. In the corner Wade has written "Friday, 8:15" and the name "Scott." Below it is an address on the other side of town and a phone number. After you finish washing the dishes but before you step into the bathroom to shower and shave, you ask Wade how his business dinner was on Friday. He flushes, surprised by your question and the fact that you remembered he was busy that evening and not with you. He answers, "It was canceled. I ended up going to a movie by myself instead."

Your sixth mistake was not asking him what movie he saw. Your seventh was that at the time you thought about asking that question, the moment of arousing his suspicion about your suspicion had passed, and you remained silent and more anxious than ever. Your eighth mistake was not dealing with your anxieties.

o   o   o

After lunch Wade kisses you when you leave his apartment, says he will see you in a few days. You say you are heading downtown to see a friend. Wade says he is spending the afternoon shopping for a new rug. This is not your first doubt or your first suspicion of the day, since you wonder if he is telling you the truth because you are convinced you have already caught him in a lie. You doubt he wants a new rug. You think he wants a new boyfriend instead, that he's going shopping for a younger, prettier, wittier, more vivacious model than you. You wonder if he is going to break up with you first or if you will break up with him first in order to protect yourself from being hurt by his breaking up with you.

On the subway ride downtown, you drift in and out of a set of clues and reasons why things are not working out between you and Wade; at the same time, you are looking around the subway car in hopes of finding other prospects for boyfriends. This leads you into thinking about the different kinds of guys you have dated over too many years. You draw them into a long list: rapper, architect, actor, insurance executive, junkie, and on and on. By the time you reach your stop, you wonder if you might be better off being single than attached to another man.

When you reach the sidewalk, you continue to cruise for

available men. You watch a tall guy jogging in sweatpants and a sweatshirt with a hood. You study the big shoes of a square-chinned, stocky man, the flash of a hairy wrist of another guy clutching his knapsack. You catch the eye of short man in a black coat with a day-old stubble of a beard. Just when you think about turning around to see if he is turning around to look at you, you realize you are at the hospital and wash away your desire to meet him.

When you reach the third floor, you find Dennis alone in his room, sitting in a chair instead of the bed. You kiss him on the forehead and listen to his cranky whine, "Don't get comfortable," he says. "I want you to go get me some applesauce." His voice is froggy, as if his vocal chords are sweating. He looks pale, his curly brown hair damp and colorless, like it has gone gray overnight.

Your first mistake was asking Dennis if there was anything else he needed from the store. Instead of answering your question, he shows you a notebook he is holding in his lap. "I've been writing down everything," he says. "It's all here. When the nurse doesn't show up, I write it down. When they let me sit in my own shit, I write it down."

You ask him again if he wants anything else from the store: juice, magazines, bottled water? He says he wants applesauce and you tell him you will be back shortly.

Outside on the sidewalk you are overwhelmed with more thoughts, this time about Dennis. You do not search for a new boyfriend. Wade has retreated to a fuzzy memory. You worry about Dennis looking pale. You worry about the strange smell you detected in his room. You worry why his friend TJ was not with him. You worry that he has been in the hospital more days this month than he has been at his apartment.

The grocery store is not crowded and you easily find the aisle where the applesauce is located. You don't remember if Dennis said he wanted sweetened or unsweetened or if he stated a preference. You look around for help but there is no one near you. Not even another shopper. You choose the plastic six-pack, unsweetened, that has "all natural" spelled out in curly red letters on top of the package. You pick up some bottled water and wait in line at the check-out counter. The line is slow-moving, every item is being hand-punched into a machine instead of being scanned. You hear the clerk—a girl with pony tails—say something is broken and explain the delay. You wait and read the headlines on the tabloids by the counter. Your second mistake was to pick up a paper and add it to your purchases when it is finally your turn at the counter.

Back in Dennis's room, your third mistake was showing him the magazine you got him. The headline reads: "Alien Invaders Sighted on Long Island." You roll your eyes and hope the story will make him laugh. He says there is nothing new about aliens on Long Island. He has aliens in his bloodstream, says he might have even gotten them on Long Island. He says the aliens in his bloodstream have been making him shit fire now for twenty-four hours. He say it like a headline—"Faggot Shits Fire!"—then decides it is clever enough to write down in his notebook.

"I want this all published when I go," he says, waving the notebook with his arm. He uses a lot of energy with the movement. His mouth opens like he is panting. You want to ask him where he thinks he's going, to try to counter his dark mood with a lighter comment, but since it didn't work before with the headline you just keep your mouth shut. Dennis is supposed to be the funny one, the one who makes you laugh. That is the way it has been since you met; the way your friendship has played itself out for years. Dennis is the funny one and you are supposed to laugh. Just when you decide you must say something—just as you are about to ask him if he wants to look at the fashion spread of worst-dressed celebrities in the centerfold, he says he wants you to help him to the bathroom, the aliens are making him shit again. He laughs at himself as he tries to turn his predicament into comedy. "The aliens have decided they want a nicer host."

You help him maneuver a few steps with the IV pole and tubes hooked into his arm. He twists himself into the small bathroom at the end of his room, asks you to untie the knot at the back of his neck where the hospital gown hangs by a string. His bottom is exposed to you. His ass is thin, shaky, strangely red and blotchy. You untie the strings and the gown slips down his arms, hangs limply on the IV tube. He sits on the toilet and makes a little groan. You want to close the door of the tiny bathroom, to give him some privacy, but his IV unit is too large, so you move to the chair where he was sitting and straighten some books that are piled on the floor.

He shits and groans and you break out into a light sweat trying to pretend you are in another room. This was your fourth mistake. You pick up his journal off the floor, look through the pages. There are drawings of cocks and butts, lists of things that Dennis likes and despises. On one page he has drawn the diagram of an anal wart and the cross-section of a butt plug. The detail is both amazing and alarming. On another page he has depicted himself giving an urine sample. Toward the back of the journal is a list of hospital cooked meals he has not eaten, mostly a list of vegetables with adjectives like "day old," "wormy" and "stale" in front of them.

He calls out to you for help and you lean into the bathroom and help him stand. The smell is overwhelming. His backside is filthy and you tell him to stay put. You find a towel, wet a corner of it with warm water, and clean his ass. He does not fight you as you wash him; instead, his face breaks into a weak smile from the attention. His cock dangles and flops and you pretend not to notice that he cups himself while you rinse him off and dry him with another towel. When you help him back into the hospital gown he is reluctant to let go of himself. When he does you notice he has become lightly aroused.

Back in the room, now in the bed, he tells you he has not been sleeping well and it is all down in his book. "I've got to write it down so that everyone knows what hell is like." He says he dreams people are sticking him with needles. Men with white hospital jackets. Needles as big as dildos.

He writes something else down into the journal, then abruptly closes the notebook. He looks at you with large, wet eyes. He says he's sorry about being so self-centered and asks you not to be mad at him. "What's happening with you?" he asks. "What's been going on?"

Your fifth mistake was answering, "Nothing."

He launches into a tirade of the loss of his freedom. His face becomes flushed and he complains he has no mobility—he cannot go see a movie and he is a prisoner of a metal pole that is taller than he is. "Something must be happening out there," he says. "Are you still dating that guy? What was his name?"

"I still see him," you answer. Dennis only knows small details about Wade. For the last year you have avoided telling Dennis too many things about your relationship. You never expected Wade to last this long. You expected Dennis to get better, not worse. Now it seems wrong for you to tell a dying friend that you are falling in love with a man who wants to fall in love with somebody else.

"Is this serious?" he asks. "Or is this still a sex-thing?"

You realize that you cannot answer him. You feel yourself shutting down, closing up, like you're guilty your life is not an open book for Dennis to read and discover who you really are. You wipe the sweat from your brow, thinking your life is one big list of mistakes, a string of things you keep doing wrong. Just when you are about to crack open and tell him a few things you are relieved to see TJ standing at the door with a grocery bag in his arm. You watch him enter the room, kiss Dennis on the lips, then kiss you on the cheek. He draws Dennis easily into a conversation about an accident on the subway, says he heard two versions of the story on his way downtown—the first was of a man being pushed into the path of a train; the second was where the man tried to stop someone else from leaping.

When Dennis decides he must write both versions of the story down in his journal, you stand and say that you will visit again tomorrow. Dennis stops writing and stretches out his journal in your direction. He says he wants you to keep it, that you have to find someone to publish what he has written down.

He pushes the journal into your hands. The gesture embarrasses you. You see it also makes TJ uneasy. Your next mistake was telling Dennis he's not finished with the journal, that he has to keep it because he might want to write something else in it tonight, or tomorrow morning, before you return to the hospital. You hand him back the journal and tell him you'll bring him a new one when you visit him tomorrow, that there are plenty more things he has to add to *this* journal. He seems to accept this idea, and the both of you look at TJ for approval. TJ seems to nod, then grow anxious himself, as if something else is on his mind. Dennis says he did not write down the dildo dream and he begins to describe it in detail to TJ.

Your seventh mistake was interrupting Dennis to kiss him good-bye. You kiss him on the lips to show him you are not scared. His stale breath stays in your mouth, like a badly digested meal.

o   o   o

The next thing you did wrong was to walk thirty-four blocks back to your apartment instead of taking the subway. The cold wind made your eyes burn, your throat felt scratchy and sore, the six-floor climb to your apartment left you winded and breathless. Inside your apartment, it was stuffy and overheated. You thought you would catch on fire before you shed your coat. Steam leaked out of the radiators with an ominous hissing sound. Everything felt like it was against you, not giving you shelter.

The next thing you did wrong was thinking that you could relax, get rid of the idea that you were still in motion. The third thing you did wrong was to turn on the television, thinking the sound would provide you comfort instead of aggravation.

The one thing you did right was drinking a glass of cold water. It seemed to help with your anxiety for a moment, until it made you think of the soggy waffles still in your stomach, now floating around in a deeper layer of fluid.

In the bathroom you washed your face with warm water, brushed your teeth a little longer than you usually do. The next thing you did wrong was notice that there was blood when you spit into the sink. You watched the tiny little string of red wash down the drain. You wondered if the brushing irritated your gums or if your mouth was decaying before the toothbrush invaded it. You rinsed your mouth with cold water, smiled in the mirror, pressed your fingertips against your gums, and drew more blood.

The next thing you did wrong was remember the sex you had with Wade the night before. You kissed him. You sucked his cock and he sucked yours. You cannot remember if you fucked him first or if he fucked you first, but you do remember that neither time was with a condom. He wanted you to come inside him, which you did. He wanted to come inside you, which he did.

The next thing you did wrong was remember Dennis's stale breath. After that you remembered that Wade was not at his apartment today. According to you, he was out shopping for a new boyfriend.

The next thing you did wrong was to dial Wade's number and leave a message on his answering machine. You asked him to call you tonight when he returned back to his apartment. You used your pleasant voice, so it would not alert Wade that you were ready for a confrontation. Wade wants to be pampered and not confronted, which is why things are so sorry for you and not safe for anyone. The biggest thing you did wrong was to wait for him to return your call. You watched the digital clock change numbers, slowly becoming bigger numbers digit by digit by digit. You listed more reasons and found more clues to be sorry. You remembered the last time you were tested for HIV and it was too long ago to offer any comfort for your bleeding gums.

The next thing you did wrong was to watch a horror movie on television, thinking that a variety of characters struggling in a burning building would erase your own sense of discomfort and dismay.

o   o   o

The first part of your dream is about a yellow post-it. You pull it out of the trash and show it to Dennis. Dennis says in his froggy voice that this is not the worst thing that can happen. He shows you a drawing of the worst thing that can happen, a nurse can insert a tube as wide as a garden hose into the urethra of your penis. Dennis shows you another drawing—a man wearing a long jacket holding a dildo—and then flips through more pages in his journal. You realize you are looking for a drawing of Wade having sex with another man and you cannot find what page you saw it on before. You take the journal away from Dennis and flip through the pages.

When the phone rings you realize that you are dreaming and you groggily rise out of the bed, much like a vampire looking for blood, and mute the sound of the television with your fist and reach for the receiver of the phone. You think it is Wade calling you back, returning your call. Instead, you are surprised to hear it is Dennis. Dennis tells you in his froggy voice that he needs the journal back, that he wants to draw the aliens that he heard pushed a man off a subway platform and into the path of an oncoming train.

He asks you again for the journal. He says he needs the journal back. You fight to give him an answer but feel dizzy, breathless from climbing so many stairs. You open your mouth but you cannot make a sound. Aliens have robbed you of your voice and you cannot tell Dennis you are now in trouble yourself.

He asks you what's wrong, where's the journal? "What's going on?"

When the phone rings again, while you are still on the phone with Dennis, you realize you are dreaming the first phone call and reach out for the phone.

Your voice is froggy when you say, "Hello." It takes you a moment to realize that you are awake, that TJ is on the other end of the phone, not Dennis, and that Wade has still not returned your call.

"I'm sorry," TJ says. "I wanted you to hear it from me first."

He tells you that Dennis died about an hour ago. He is still at the hospital. There are things that still have to be done. He is waiting for someone to come to the room. He has to pack some stuff up and go uptown to Dennis's apartment.

You are at a loss of words but you find yourself saying, "Sorry," and asking for more details. TJ explains something about a valve of the heart not working properly and he says he will call you tomorrow. Before he hangs up he starts crying, says he will give you the journal in a few days because he wants to read through it first.

When he hangs up you stare at the picture on the television. The horror movie is no longer there. You watch a commercial where a young woman runs through a field of yellow flowers towards a tall, slender man with eyeglasses who is walking a golden retriever. You think they are all aliens. Your life is nothing like this.

You look at the bright red digital numbers of the clock beside your bed and decide that it is too late for Wade to call you back. It is already the next day. You turn off the television and the room floats into darkness.

The first thing that makes you afraid is that the room is dark and you have lost your vision. The second thing that frightens you is that your throat feels rough and scratchy. The third thing that worries you is your uncertainty about your health. But your biggest fear is the one you cannot let go of. You are in love and now feel lonelier than you ever did when you were single. You can't even tell Dennis how miserable you are. The next thing you worry about is what you should do next. Your sixth worry is that you will not fall back asleep. And your next one is feeling you no longer want to remain awake.

What You Find

He kisses you on the lips and says good-bye in a whisper. As you hear the door click shut behind him you are suddenly wide awake, aware of the morning stillness in his apartment. This is the first time you have been left alone in his apartment after seven months of dating him, sleeping over occasionally at his apartment on the weekends, and you stretch your legs out in the bed, tensing the sleep out of your muscles. You feel the space where he slept last night next to you, still warm, you think, then run the palm of your hand over the flat empty space of the sheet and draw his pillow up to your face, breathing in the remaining scent of him. You think a moment about last night's sex, feeling yourself getting hard. You play with yourself for a moment, slipping your hand beneath your underwear, stroking yourself, then cupping your balls. You sigh loudly and get out of bed.

In the kitchen you make coffee, fiddle with yourself in your underwear some more, wanting to keep yourself semierect and edgy as long as you can. You sit at the table and eat a cranberry muffin he bought for you at the grocery store yesterday. You look at the digital clock on the VCR. It reads 9:17. You calculate he won't be back for another four hours—gone to his daughter's graduation in Connecticut. You don't know what amazes you more—the fact that he is forty-nine years old and has a daughter old enough to graduate high school, or the fact that he is still married and filing for a divorce. *Another married man trying to escape his past without regrets.*

You glance outside the window as you chew on your muffin,

happy as you taste the burst of a cranberry in your mouth. You stare at the trees in the park across the street, the tops of which are puddles of deep green leaves. He says he's gay, though he won't admit it to anyone except you and the tricks he meets at his favorite bar on the East Side. He's not told his soon-to-be-ex-wife the reason why their marriage is ending, hasn't told his daughter why he no longer lives at home. He has no plans to come out on the job, no plans, either, for you, except to have sex when his schedule permits. He doesn't want a relationship, after all, you remind yourself—only someone to have a good time with. That's all you want out of this too, you tell yourself, but you know that's not true. You've spent the last two decades of your adult life looking for a lover, and just when you found someone you want to fall in love with—just when you are ready—he tells you he wants to date other people and doesn't want to settle down.

The story of my life, you think with a big sigh. You get up from the table. You wash your coffee mug in the kitchen sink and place it in the dish rack. You wonder why he has left you alone in his apartment—after months and months of insinuating that he was dating other men, that you weren't the *only* distraction in his life, that he knew you were the possessive and jealous type, did he think that you had changed after all this time? Or has he changed, you wonder? Is he ready for a relationship now? No, you remind yourself again. It's sex, not a relationship. You're just fuck buddies who go to the movies together.

At least it's good, you think. The sex. At least you find him sexy. At least he appreciates you appreciating him. At least it makes you feel good to make him feel good. Well, most of the time. You walk out of the kitchen and again are drawn to the view from his window. The light is bright this morning and you cast your eyes downward, following the tiny figure of a jogger in an orange sweatshirt as he enters the park from the street. Before he left you alone you had made up your mind you wouldn't snoop through his things—you knew enough about him already, and what you suspected of him you didn't need confirmed. You're thirty-nine years old. You're a mature, open, honest gay man. You don't need to snoop through a married boyfriend's stuff. You don't need your jealousy piqued, your possessiveness inflamed. You already have enough problems with this pseudo-relationship—his age, his marriage, his money, his ego.

You suddenly smack yourself in the head with the palm of your hand, listening to the sound it makes. *Why, why, why are you here?* you ask yourself. Are you that desperate for attention? That needy for *any* kind of relationship? *Yes*, you answer. You're such a fool. And Keith's dead. So are Dennis and Tony and Greg and a lot of those other boys you used to play with. Peter thinks he is in a relationship now. And then there is Jack. Emotionally unavailable Jack. *Why do you keep falling for the same sort of guy over and over?*

You turn on the television and check the weather on NY1—the box in the corner reads sixty-nine degrees. You turn up the sound so that you can hear it above the stereo and wait for the newscaster to read the forecast, running your finger across the head of your cock. The newscaster predicts that it may reach the high eighties today. You stand in front of the TV playing with yourself, looking out again at the view, this time looking at the rows of buildings that frame the other end of the park. You think about him sucking your cock, then think about sucking his cock, then imagine him on the couch with his legs apart, and you feel yourself grow harder, frustrated. You fight off the urge to masturbate—he's coming back, you know, and he'll want to have sex—and so will you. You surf through the channels with the remote control, lingering for a moment on a wrestling program, admiring the body of one of the wrestlers—thick and muscled about the arms and shoulders. You wish for a moment he had a better body. Wish he were younger and better looking. You wish he were the wrestler. You're still hard and you squeeze your cock now, stroke it back and forth really good a few times, then click the TV off with the remote just when you're ready to want more. You switch on the stereo and begin stretching your neck, twist your waist back and forth and side to side until you feel loose, supple, and awake.

You turn the stereo up louder and wander into the bedroom. You slip on his sneakers, hoping you'll stretch them out of shape. You laugh. Your feet are bigger than his. But he has the bigger waist. You look at yourself in the mirror over his dresser. You look better than you have in the last ten years. You've lost fifteen pounds since you've started dating him—anxiety over trying to make it work for you, too, you know. But it has made you look younger, more attractive, you think. You certainly notice you get more looks now on the street. And you never walk out of a bar alone these days. You stare at your waist. Twenty-nine inches. You can even see the muscles in your stomach. You couldn't when you were twenty-nine years old.

You turn on the treadmill in the corner of the room, start walking at a slow pace. You turn up the speed, punch the reset button. Your erection drops off fast as the pace of your feet gets faster and faster. Even if he doesn't want you someone else will. Even if this ends there will be someone else. He's not the only person you're seeing. Your little joke on him. *As if he even cared*, you think. You walk and walk, noticing the furniture in his bedroom. You remember when they delivered the dresser. You suggested he get the mission-style headboard because it would work well with handcuffs. You were with him when he bid on the Hockney at Christie's.

You notice an unfamiliar envelope on the top of the dresser and it disturbs you. You don't know what it is. You think about stopping the treadmill to snoop, but you don't. You keep walking, turning the speed up even faster.

He'll never lose the weight, you remind yourself. He eats too much junk—snacks and cookies throughout the day, every night potato chips, chocolate ice cream, and a carafe of wine before going to bed. How does he do it—consume so much food? You don't even have an appetite anymore. All you want is to feel good about something. All you ask from him is some kind of affection, which is the last thing he is willing to give.

You stop after thirty-one minutes and two-and-a-half miles. You are drenched in sweat. Your cock is small, wet. You get off the treadmill and check the envelope on top of the dresser. It is the invitation to his daughter's graduation ceremony. You look at the clock. Two hours and forty minutes left. He could get back early, though. You lie on the floor and look at the ceiling, then force yourself through one hundred crunches. You roll over and lie on your stomach, lift yourself up into a position for push-ups. Your feet slide against his polished wooden floor. You inch your way down till the heels of your feet are against the bottom drawer of his night stand. You do fifty push-ups and then rest. You make a note in your head to remind him to invest in a chin-up bar. He will never do it, you know. It would ruin the aesthetics of his apartment. You do fifty more push-ups, purposely banging your heels against his dresser drawer. That's where he keeps the dildos and lube. Where the condoms come from. Where he stashes the magazines he picks up at the bar.

You roll over and open the drawer and look inside. *Oh hell*, you think, *you've started snooping. Just find it all out and get it over with.* You've seen all the toys in this drawer before. Three sizes of dildos—thin, regular, and extra big with a double head. Nothing is new that you can tell except the recent issue of *Next* which is dated this weekend. That means he went to the bar this week.

You close the drawer and sit on the bed. You untie his sneakers and throw them on top of the treadmill. You open the top drawer of the night stand. You've never seen him open this drawer. On top are his pay stubs. You read the year-to-date earnings column. You estimate he makes close to $400,000 a year. You are stunned. You had no idea he made *that* much. He did say once that he made more money than a doctor. Then you get angry. You pay for half of everything you do together—the movies, the theater tickets, the occasional restaurant, the trip last month to Boston for the weekend. You barely make $25,000 a year. You try to shrug it off, but you can't. He once told you he would like you more if you made more money. *Jerk*, you think. *Pig.* All he's after is sex. All he wants is a good time. He's just using you. Using you for the sex. And you're not even getting paid for it.

You look through the rest of the drawer. There are scraps of paper with numbers and addresses written on them. You read each one. John at a Chelsea phone number, Paul on East 80th Street. There is another pile of business cards he must have gotten from tricks at the bar. You become perturbed because there are so many of them. You even find one of your old boyfriends in his pile. Small world, you try to console yourself, then laugh because you think they both deserve each other. *They're both jerks,* you tell yourself. *Both nothing but pigs.*

In the back of the drawer you notice a membership card to the East Side baths. You look at the expiration date and are relieved that it expired one month before you started dating him. *What a pig I've found,* you tell yourself again. Why would you want to be in a relationship with a sex junkie? Why has this affair lasted this long?

You shake your head. That's not what you want. You wonder if he will ever want to settle down. He was up-front when you confronted him with it after you had been dating each other for six weeks. He said he just got out of a twenty-two-year marriage, why would he want to settle down with someone right away? You remind yourself that it was your choice to continue this. Then you remind yourself that since he cheated on his wife when he was married—of course he's going to cheat around on a *boyfriend.* Then you tell yourself that "cheat" is the wrong word. There's nothing going on between the two of you, after all. At least not from his direction. It's just sex. Just dating. You close the drawer. You don't want to know any more. You try not to get upset. Don't make him into someone he's not going to be.

Pigs, you think. *They're all pigs.* Rich men, fat men, gay men. They're all jerks. Even yourself. When did you ever have a decent boyfriend? When were you ever a decent one yourself? You never told him about your ongoing thing with Jack, never mentioned the ad you placed in *HX* two months ago, never mentioned the string of blind dates you had, never mentioned whom you met on the phone lines. *But he provoked it*, you tell yourself. Didn't he *make* you look by reminding you of your every imperfection over and over? That you are far from the perfect boyfriend for him? That you weren't rich enough or young enough or cute enough or hot enough? And weren't you just hoping to find someone better than *him*?

You go into the kitchen and get a drink of water. You look at your watch. Ninety more minutes. You could read the book you brought, look through the notes of your novel that you think will never be finished. Suddenly you are aware that you will never have any money. You're a struggling writer, you write short stories, you write about gay life. You will never have this kind of money. You look back at the view of Central Park. If you give him up you will never see this view again. But you would never feel this lousy again, either.

When you first started dating him all you did was have sex. Sex in his new bed, sex in the kitchen, sex on the ottoman, sex on the floor. He was so cheap, he didn't even take you out for dinner. You wonder for a moment if you had his kind of money would you be dating someone like him? No, you think. You would be out of here quick. But you don't like him for just his money. And you want him for something more than just the sex.

You remember how much you have in your wallet. Two dollars. You just paid the rent on your sixth-floor walk-up in Hell's Kitchen. You're broke. You don't even have enough to go out for a sandwich. Instead you walk into the bathroom and rinse your face. You open the medicine chest and count the number of new toothbrushes on the shelf. Four. None gone. None of the packages have been opened since you were last here. You know he keeps them for tricks. Just like he does the stack of disposable razors. You pull down a razor he has saved for you and lather your face with his shaving crème. You smile at yourself in the mirror. *Fool*, you think. You're such a clown. At least you can pretend to be happy. Maybe you should have been an actor after all and not a writer.

You shave and then brush your teeth. You look at yourself in the mirror, admire your waist, flex your biceps, then think: *Treat me nice when I'm poor and I'll love you when I'm rich.*

You walk out of the bathroom and into his closet. You smell his shirts—freshly laundered and ironed cotton button-down. You touch his jackets, wave your fingers through the rack of ties, then thumb through them for the one he bought when you went together to Barney's. You play with yourself again and realize that you are already hard.

You try on one of his shirts. It fits nicely, but you don't even contemplate trying on his pants; there's a five inch difference between your waists. You take the shirt off and look at yourself in the mirror nailed to the back of the closet door. You strike a pose. You run your hand up and down your stomach. You cup your balls, twirling the ends of your pubic hair. You would never shave your balls. You like it natural. You think about the times you've shaved his balls, the erection he gets as he's handled by you. You smile and then shake your head. *Where is all this going?* you wonder. *Right into therapy?*

You decide to explore some more. He once told you he kept cash hidden in the apartment, out of sight of his wife's lawyer. You wonder if you can find it. Suddenly, the prospect of this new game seizes you. You open his dresser drawers, looking beneath his underwear, between his T-shirts, inside his socks, through his shorts and under his slacks. You're obsessed with finding some money, any money, even if it's just a dollar bill or some coins he uses for laundry. You're not going to steal it, you just want to discover it, count it, touch it, know where it is because he makes such a big issue of how much he has and how little you have. Instead, you find a book of erotic stories under his jeans. You thumb through it. Nothing inside so you put it back. Maybe he's cash poor, you think as you close the drawer. Maybe he's just a portfolio—all stocks and assets.

The bottom drawer surprises you, however, when you open it—there is a row of neatly stacked videos. You pick one up. It is

The Best of Joey Stefano. You look at the photo of the guy on the cover. Dark hair, dark eyes, unshaven pouty looks. You've seen him on the reruns on Robin Byrd's cable show a couple of times. *Didn't he die?* you think. *Didn't he have a drug problem?*

You put the video back in the drawer. You lift up another one. Same guy on the cover, full body shot, tattoo on his bicep. Joey Stefano in *Tattoo You.* You look at Joey. You look at yourself in the mirror. No contest, you think. He's younger. Hotter. Better arms. Better ass. You feel defeated. You put that video back and lift up one more. *Prince Charming,* with Joey Stefano's name in the cast list. As you turn it over an envelope falls to the ground. You pick it up and notice there is a phone number written on the front, 213 area code. California. You look inside the envelope, opening it carefully where it has been taped shut. It is full of small black hairs. Pubic hair, you think. An envelope full of pubic hair. It can't be *his*—his is gray. It must be Joey Stefano's pubic hair. *You have discovered an envelope full of Joey Stefano's pubic hair.*

What a pig you've found out you're dating. You had a big fight once over the porn. He wanted to watch it during sex. You wanted a little more attention from him. You sigh, aware that you will never be his ideal type—he's told you that, in fact. But you've never insulted him, however, never told him that you think he could lose a little weight, go to gym a little more, that the bald spot at the back of his head really *does* reflect light. But then you're easier than he is. You're not so specific when it comes to men and body types and hair. All you want is someone to care—he doesn't have to look like a bodybuilder or a wrestler or the bouncer you once saw in front of a club. Okay, so you're jealous, you think. Deal with it. Get over it. Accept it and move on.

You go into the bathroom and flush Joey Stefano's pubic hair down the toilet. Then you open the medicine cabinet and find his nail scissors. You take off your underwear. You snip off some of your pubic hair. It is the same color as Joey's. You put it in the envelope and return it to the drawer with the videos. You kick the drawer closed with your foot, hoping you've made a dent in the wood.

You lie back on the bed again and stare at the ceiling, playing with your cock. How do you make things work, you wonder. You don't want to give up. You're not a quitter. Something is going on with this man if he trusts you enough to leave you behind in his apartment. You look at the photo of his daughter on his dresser. You could always blackmail him, you think. You could earn your fortune by threatening to expose him to his wife and his boss.

Grow up, you tell yourself. He is his own boss. And you're too old to be a double-crossing boy toy. You would never do that. You're too gay yourself, too out, too proud to even think about doing something like that. What you want is to make something work, make this relationship work. But what if this is the wrong one? What if you've picked the wrong guy again?

You squeeze your cock, rub your fist over the head. You feel yourself getting hard. You close your eyes, feel the muscles of your chest tense. You think about the guy you saw in the men's department at Bloomingdale's yesterday. Black hair, great arms. Better looking than Joey Stefano, you laugh to yourself. You imagine him going down on you. The guy at Bloomingdale's. Not Joey. You lift your legs up in the air, wet a finger in your mouth, then begin to play with your asshole. You're hot, bothered, frustrated, and worked up. You pump your cock. Harder and harder. You push two fingers into your ass. Move them in and out as you work your fist up and down your cock. When you shoot you almost hit your nipple. You open your eyes and calm your breathing. You feel mean and nasty. You take some of your come and rub it onto his comforter. You're such a pig, you think. Why are all gay men such pigs? You're no better than he is. You get up off the bed and go to the bathroom.

You piss and then step into the shower. You use his soap and shampoo. You find a clean towel and dry yourself off with it, just to make another one dirty for him to have to wash. You use his cologne and deodorant. You dry your hair with his hair dryer. You smell like him, you think, as you admire yourself in his mirror. He's all over you.

You look at the clock. He'll be back in about five minutes. Your heart begins to beat faster. You take a deep breath and hurriedly put on your jeans and sweatshirt, sitting on the couch and lacing up your boots. You get your jacket out of the closet. You take a last look at his view.

Then you leave. You open the door and just walk out, listening to it slam behind you. He will never find your jealousy, anger, and obsession again, you decide. And he will not find you in his apartment when he returns.

Who is Us?

"What about that one?" Jack asks.

You know he is talking about the blue shirt, but you can't help notice him noticing the attractive, young salesman behind the counter who holds it up.

"I've seen better," you answer, thinking your answer covers all bases—the blue shirt and the young man. "But I'm sure you would look perfect with it."

"Not me," Jack answers. "*You.* I think it's time you invest in a better one."

"I love my shirt," you say. "It's my favorite."

Jack hates the shirt you are wearing. It is a light blue cotton shirt with a button-down collar that has been washed so many times it is as soft as cashmere. It is over eleven years old and too large for you. You got it the first weekend you spent with Jack because it once belonged to him. Jack believes that when you wear this shirt you are doing a poor imitation of him, or worse, that you trying to mock him and his lifestyle. At the large house in the suburbs where Jack lives with his wife of twenty-four years, he has a closet full of shirts just like your favorite one, all hand-made and tailored to fit him.

"My treat," Jack says to you, hoping to show the young salesman that he is a magnanimous, if older, catch. "Let me get you a new shirt so you can get rid of that one."

"No," you answer. "The shirt is not the problem."

Jack does not hate your favorite shirt because it is out of style. He hates it because it is falling apart; the cuffs are frayed and the button placket is so worn down that the threads are beginning to unravel. Jack is as vain about his clothing as he is about his hairline; he is an impeccable dresser, even his jeans have creases. Jack thinks the shirt makes you look like a starving pauper. He is more appalled by the condition of your favorite blue shirt than by the frayed knees of your jeans or the split ends of your cowlick. Many times, during last decade or so, he has offered to give you one of his new shirts if you will just stop wearing this old blue one when you get together with him. You had actually thought about tossing the shirt out at the end of summer, the last time you saw Jack. Already it is late November.

"Why are you being so stubborn?" Jack asks, when he has given up on impressing the young salesman and has followed you outside the store. You know Jack is no longer talking about the shirt. As you start walking uptown he quickens his pace to walk beside you. "Why are you doing this?"

"I want to give it a chance."

"What about us?" he asks.

"What do you mean?" you ask. You stop walking and look at him. His forehead is creased with lines. "I see you three, four times a year. There is no *us*."

"What makes you so certain that this one is going to work out?" Jack asks.

"Instinct," you answer. "It just feels right. You remember how that works, don't you?"

You wait to see if he is stupid enough to ask what is wrong with the way things are with him—with you and him. Instead, he surprises you and asks, "Do you love him?"

That word, the word you've been searching for years to hear someone say to you, sounds garbled in Jack's mouth. In fact, it sounds so strange in his mouth that you stop and wonder if you have ever heard him say it before. Well, Jack has said he loves caramel-covered popcorn and he loves going to the beach, but that is not the same as talking about love. That is not the same word that has just sounded garbled in his mouth.

"Not yet," you answer, "but I'm on my way to it," and your answer makes Jack reach his arm out to touch you at the wrist, something he never does in public—touching you, out in the street, where people can see the kind of man he really is.

"How long has this been going on?" he asks. There is a desperation in his voice that has never been there before, in the more than eleven years you have been wearing this shirt and seeing Jack on an occasional basis.

"A few months," you answer. "Five months to be exact. I met him at a bar in June."

"But you said he had a lover," Jack says. "I remember you talking about him. You said he was in a relationship."

"They broke up," you answer. "But his lover hasn't moved out yet."

"So it's not the end of us," Jack says as if he has discovered a set of lost car keys and the worry is over.

"*Us*?" you echo. "Who is *us*?"

o   o   o

These are the facts: You are forty years old and still looking for a decent relationship. You have a new boyfriend named Adam, aged forty-seven, who has recently broken up with his lover of eight years. Adam wants to see you every weekend but doesn't want to get too serious too soon. You also have Jack. Jack is fifty-seven and looks a decade younger than his age; you've been having sex with him for more than eleven years. Over time, Jack has turned into a good listener, or, rather, you have turned Jack into a good listener because he is self-involved and he believes himself to be "involved" with you because he has continued to see you for sex and an occasional dinner or a clandestine road trip. When you see Jack two or three times a year, you tell him about your bad dates, bad affairs, and bad relationships, which also includes the time you spend with him—you tell him exactly how self-focused he is and he gets a good laugh out of this because he considers himself to be one of the best things in your life; in retaliation to your confessions and insults, he tells you about the younger tricks he's met at a bar or in his suburban grocery store. Jack has made it clear that he will never leave his wife and that he does not care to get serious about you even though he believes he is seriously "involved" with you because of the passage of so much time. Every time you see Jack you make a promise that this will be the last time with him but you never completely break things off. You have a hard time taking Jack seriously, too.

Jack stops in front of a store window where shiny black shoes are lined up on shelves. He pretends to look at the shoes but you know he is looking at the reflection of himself in the window. Jack is vain. *Very* vain. But he is so handsome that you often regard his vanity as well deserved. Jack is convinced that the reason why you are trying to become more serious with Adam is because he—Jack—is rapidly aging. Jack spends a fortune hiding his thick, gray hair with a strange brown-orange color he finds at a hair salon not far from this shop window.

"Do you think I should get my eyes done?" Jack asks.

"You have beautiful eyes. Why would you change them?"

"No," he says. "A little tuck. And around the neck, too."

You laugh and walk away from him. "I think it would ruin your looks," you say. "And it's the one thing you've got going for you."

He studies himself as best he can in the shifting light, finds it hard to leave his reflection and catch up with you. "How could you want to give this up?" he asks. "Don't you know how good I am for you?"

"It's not like we would stop talking to each other," you say.

"What? And be just friends?" he says. "After what we just did?"

These are some more facts: This afternoon, after sex with Jack at your apartment, you suggested to him that it was becoming more difficult to see him, not because you wanted or expected to be monogamous with Adam but because you wanted to let go of the psychological weight of Jack: Jack knows about Adam but

Adam does not know about Jack. Jack immediately seized on this dishonesty of your new arrangement—Adam can have a lover, even if the lover has now become an ex-one, he pointed out, but you must arrive and exist in this new relationship without a past. You countered that Jack was one to lecture about honesty—his wife has known nothing about you for the eleven-plus years you have been seeing Jack.

Now, on the way to have dinner before Jack heads back to his wife and the suburbs, Jack has stopped in front of another store window to look at shirts. You know that this is another test for you. He wants to see if you will stop beside him or continue on, just leave him on the street like a crumpled up candy wrapper like you have often threatened to do to him because of his lack of any kind of decent commitment to you.

He knows you too well. And that your threats are idle. You stop at his shoulder and look at the shop window.

"Do you like that tie?" he asks. "I think it might go with my new gray suit."

"I've never seen your new suit," you answer. "But it is a beautiful tie."

o   o   o

At the restaurant, a table comes easily even though you arrive without a reservation. The waitress thinks Jack is a celebrity, but she cannot quite place him, so she seats the two of you near the window. Jack orders a steak and fries, even though he is worried about his weight and his waist. You are more sensible, ordering a salad and grilled salmon.

"I think you can do better," Jack says.

You know he is not talking about the food. "You don't even know him."

"You met him at a bar," he says. "You told me so yourself."

You take a sip of your glass of wine and look away from Jack because he chews and talks at the same time. Outside the window, a couple stops and looks at the menu at the side of the door. You feel like you should yell at them and warn them to go away: this restaurant is only full of dishonest people in deceitful relationships who don't know what they are talking about.

"Never expect a relationship from a guy you meet at a bar," Jack says. "He only wants one of two things. To get drunk. Or to get laid. And most of the time the second reason is the one that counts."

"I met you at a bar," you answer, though you do not complete your thought out loud—that after almost twelve years Jack still does not want a relationship with you because, the truth of the matter is, he likes stringing you on, knowing that you will see him when he calls. You can only insult Jack so much without him wearing the hurt on his handsome face, which only makes him more appealing. And needy. And you all the more interested in him because of the two.

He smiles, at first as though he has been trapped into a position he doesn't like. Then his eyes brighten, as if he has found a weakness in your response. "I'm your one exception," he says and widens his smile.

A young, boyish-looking waiter arrives with your salad and you notice him exchange glances with Jack. Anger flashes through your mind until you remind yourself that nothing is going on here of any consequence—at least not between you and Jack. After eleven years, there are probably hundreds of men between you and Jack and you refuse to let a slim-waisted waiter provoke your frustration further.

"If he cheats on his lover he's gonna cheat on you," Jack says.

"They've broken up," you remind him, watching the waiter move through the room and stop at another table.

"He wasn't single when you met him, was he?" Jack asks.

The waiter arrives again and fills Jack's water glass. There is a moment when his crotch is against the edge of the table. Jack pretends that nothing is going on. You pretend that the waiter has not forgotten to fill your water glass and hope the distraction will change the topic of conversation. It doesn't.

"Do you think you're the only person he has met at a bar?" Jack asks.

"Why are you trying to spoil this?"

"Why are you trying to ruin us?" Jack answers.

"*Us*?" you shoot back. "Who is *us*?"

o   o   o

These are more facts: Adam is as imperfect and self-absorbed as Jack. He is tall and rangy with curly soft hair. Adam is not as handsome as Jack is but he is more accessible, at least at the moment. And, according to your math, he is richer than Jack but only because he has not spent his income on a wife and two kids and a suburban home, though the size of his wealth is unimportant to you. Once, a couple of weeks ago, you thought that giving up Jack for Adam was like deciding you wanted a yellow apple instead of a red one. Apples for apples is how you figured it all out when the thought occurred to you that maybe you shouldn't give Jack up, which only makes what Jack says about Adam at the restaurant hit too close to the truth.

"Does he love you like I love you?" Jack says when dessert arrives.

There is that garbled sound again. "Now you are being mean," you answer.

"When is it mean to tell someone you care about him?" Jack says.

"Because you don't care. Not that way."

"That's not true," Jack says. "You mean a lot to me."

"I'm a convenience to you until I'm inconvenient," you answer.

Even though you have seen Jack for more than eleven years he is still a transient in your life. You are not allowed to call him. You are not allowed to speak to him at home or at the office. You only get together when Jack wants to get together, when Jack is ready to see you. While you think about this, you sense it all boiling inside of you, upsetting your stomach. "I can't even call you," you finally blurt out.

"Is that what you want?" he asks. "You can call me whenever you want to call me if that's what you need."

The waiter interrupts again and sets cups and saucers in front of your places.

"That's not what I want," you say. The waiter returns with a coffee pot. He pours Jack's cup first, then yours. While he is pressing his crotch against the edge of the table he overfills your cup. When you try to pull the cup away, the coffee spills onto your shirt. The waiter apologizes and hands you a cloth napkin. You dab at the growing stain, then decide to leave the two of them together to wash it out in the restroom.

In the bathroom you stare at the stain in the mirror. As you wet the fabric it rips once, and then again. You knew this was going to happen. There was no way to prevent it. The shirt is now in threads. You stand in front of the mirror and wonder why. *Why? Why? Why have you let this happen?*

You are not thinking at all about the shirt.

o   o   o

Back at the table Jack is putting something into his wallet. You know it is not his credit card; the bill is still on the table. When you take your seat he does not notice that you have tied the blue shirt around your waist nor that your white T-shirt has been stained with coffee, too.

"There was a lady two tables over that kept looking at me," Jack says. "You couldn't see her because your back was to her. She thought I was an actor. When you left she came over and asked me if I ever did commercials. She gave me her card. She's some kind of agent."

"Did you tell her you had plenty of experience?"

"Doing what?" he asks. "What are you talking about?"

"Acting," you answer. "That you've had plenty of experience being an actor. That you are, in fact, quite good at it. That you are not at all the man you appear to be."

"Now you are being mean," he says.

The boyish waiter arrives and apologizes again. Jack withdraws his wallet once more and hands him a credit card. "My treat," he says, puffing up his chest and showing off his largesse to the waiter.

When the waiter leaves, Jack says to you, "I love spending time with you. I love when we get together."

You think he is actually telling you the truth. "But?" you answer.

"No buts," he says. "I just don't like losing."

o   o   o

On the walk back to the garage where Jack has parked his car you imagine the city as a movie set—the honking traffic disappears, the woman screaming out a second-story window to a man on the sidewalk is not there, the neon lights become a bit brighter, more romantic. You imagine Jack taking your hand and pulling you to a stop, drawing his arms around your waist and pressing his beautiful, handsome face into yours for a lingering kiss. Instead, he walks slightly ahead of you as he always does. When you must stop at a corner before crossing the street, he says, "Do you realize how much we've been through together?"

The sentiment surprises you. Then angers you. "We've not been together," you say. "You've been through stuff and I've been through stuff."

"I've always been there for you," he says.

"No," you answer. "You've been around. There is a difference."

At the garage you wait with him while an attendant locates his car. The walk is over. And you are beginning to feel tired.

"I've always wanted to go to Hawaii," he says, when the attendant has driven his car to the front space and is holding the car door open for Jack. "You know, I've never been to Hawaii. We could take a trip together. I bet I could rummage up some frequent-flyer points and we could go for a trip to Hawaii."

"What would you tell Colleen?"

"I wouldn't have to tell her anything," he says. "Isn't that what you want? You don't really want me around you all the time, do you? That would only drive you crazy. No, make that crazier."

He grins at the thought of making a joke.

"Why is it that you are so determined to continue this after all these years of not being that determined about it? Because I need some space?"

You are now waiting for him to leave, waiting for him to get in his car and drive away, back to the life he has when he is not anywhere near you or thinking of you.

"Because that's not the way it has to be," he says. "What did you expect me to do? Let you just walk out on a good thing? I've invested a lot of time in you."

He gets into his car and starts the engine. He rolls down the window, a power window using a tiny electric knob on his door.

"Can I give you a lift somewhere?" he asks. "Let me take you where you want to be. One last time, for old times sake."

You open the car door and slip inside.

"Welcome to my chariot of love," he says.

"Stop fooling around," you say in a rather serious way.

"Who's fooling whom?" he answers, in a not-so-serious tone of voice.

He edges the car out into the traffic and you look out the window. After a few blocks the city drops away. Once again, it is just you and him.

What is Everything?

After work you walk to the bookstore. It is autumn, your favorite time of year. The air has changed. Everything seems sharper, clearer; easier to detect and observe. You can see the sky between the buildings, the windows of the buildings, the ads on the top of taxis and the sides of buses, the buttons on a stranger's jacket. You can see deeper into things than any other time of the year, everything seems to have a logic, or at least you think you have an understanding of things, perhaps, because autumn is the season you were born in.

You have been working here, in this tall building for nine months. Eight hours a day you type and copy and file. It is not challenging work but it drains you of energy nonetheless. The city, the light autumn air, the details of buildings and the way the setting sun hits them invigorates you. You started walking to the bookstore after work in spring when the weather began to get warmer, then continued when you moved in with Adam six weeks ago because it was on your walk home. The heat and mugginess of the summer have finally gone; you are not looking forward to finding your old winter coat in a few weeks.

The bookstore is crowded. Vacation is over; time shares and summer houses are through though the usual large group is by the travel section. One girl sits cross-legged on the floor to read, oblivious of others reaching over her head. You lose your focus the deeper you walk into the store, uncertain whether you want to look at the fiction shelves or the magazines. You stop and adjust your backpack on your shoulder. A few steps lead you to a shelf of anthologies. You scan the titles, pull one off the shelf. A few minutes later you are sitting at a table in the back, sipping at a cup of too hot coffee and pretending to read.

o o o

At home, Adam is at his desk, typing at his keyboard. He stops and shuts the computer off and walks into the living room, turning on the television to watch the news. You are part of his evening routine. You ask him if he wants a drink. Bourbon or a martini? He says bourbon and in the kitchen you fix him a drink in an etched tumbler he bought while in Palm Springs.

The apartment is huge compared to your last apartment. There is a view of the river from the living room and a kitchen with a dishwasher, though it is seldom used. There is a hallway of walk-in closets and two full baths and two bedrooms, one which you share to sleep in and the other where Adam works. Adam retired six months ago at the beginning of the summer, a decade and a half away from being a senior citizen but rich enough from a banking career to no longer need to work. He spends his day on the Internet now, checking on his investments and checking out chat rooms. Though he talked about moving to the west coast or Florida, he decided to stay in the city for a while longer. His decision to retire prompted his decision to ask you to move in after his ex-lover finally moved out.

You bring Adam his drink. He likes to be pampered, though he is not as co-dependent as some of your previous boyfriends. When you sit down on the couch Adam says that you should not get too comfortable. He is starving and ready to go out to eat as soon as he finishes his drink. You eat out almost every night. This is one of the perks of living with Adam. He doesn't like to eat at home anymore and he pays the bill at whatever restaurant he chooses.

Tonight the restaurant is Italian. There is a piped in Renaissance music and candles at the table. There is a sense of romance in the room though not at your table. Adam gets gnocchi with a white cream sauce; you have a chicken dish because you are fighting off eating out too much. Your energy comes back as you eat. You explain that tomorrow, Friday, you will be home late from work. You have to finish a mailing and will not be done until late. Adam nods vigorously to dismiss the explanation. Actually, he doesn't like conversation at dinner. The food he eats is so delicious and so rich, he doesn't want to be distracted from it. The few times you eat at the apartment he reads the paper while he chews, unless there is something on television he would rather watch.

After dinner you walk through your neighborhood. Adam does not talk much except to point something out that catches his attention. You don't mind, really, you use the time to look and think. The city is always at its best in autumn, you think. On nights like this you could live in this city forever. Everything looks perfect, even the scaffolding around the building being constructed seems pretty and delicate.

Adam suggests renting a movie tonight, so you walk together to the video store, help Adam look through titles, then return home, finally glad to be out of your shoes.

o   o   o

At the bookstore, you sip coffee and read. The coffee is hot and strong and you wish you had gotten decaffeinated. The book is not interesting. You should have gotten something out of the ordinary, like a book of mysteries or an encyclopedia on gardening. The mailing was finished early, so early you left work hours before the day ended. Outside, the sky was cloudy, not clear. It looked like rain and you did not bring an umbrella. The bookstore is crowded with people with nothing else to do on a Friday night.

Before you left for work this morning Adam mentioned he was having dinner with his friend Blake. "Tell him I said hello," you said before you left the apartment. "Tell him I want to see him before he leaves for England."

The truth is Adam is not having dinner with Blake, but lunch.

While Adam was showering last night you checked his date book: "Blake, lunch. Todd, dinner." Adam has been having an affair with Todd for close to five months, or so you have calculated. You have struggled with this knowledge since the day you discovered it, one month before Adam asked you to move in with him. If you were to confront him on it he would not think himself different from any other gay man living in the city today. Adam now has everything he wants out of gay life. A lover and a boyfriend, a companion and an affair. He sees his job now as trying to maintain this balance, of one not finding out about the other, though he is less successful at this than he is with his financial investments.

In the bookstore you try not to let this realization about your relationship overwhelm you. You consider its pluses and minuses. You have a rich lover who pays for your meals and rent. You are living in the kind of apartment you could not afford on your own: there is a doorman, a dishwasher, and a river view. The affair takes pressure off of you to always entertain and pamper Adam. Someone else shares the burden, so to speak, and you reap the benefits and perks. All in all a pretty good arrangement; all you have to do is pretend you don't care about something you are not supposed to know about.

You decide to return the book and find a science fiction anthology to read, something that will take you out of yourself, away from the bookstore and your life in your perfect apartment.

You stand in front of the shelf of books so long you lose your focus. Only when you are aware that there is someone looking over your shoulder do you shift your position, aware that you are standing too close to even read the titles.

"Sorry," you say.

"No problem," someone answers. The voice is dark, young, and full of hormones.

o   o   o

On Saturday morning your friend Peter visits. Peter has broken up with his latest boyfriend of six weeks and visits more often now. Adam and Peter always invite you to go out with them, but today you don't feel like tagging along. Peter is more your friend than Adam's, but Peter is co-dependent and needs someone to go to the gym with him and Adam is only eager to oblige. You know Adam thinks that Peter is cute. Sexy, actually, is what he thinks. "He reeks of sex," is the exact phrase Adam once used about Peter. Adam likes to hear Peter's stories about backrooms and sex clubs. You only enjoy hearing Peter's stories when Adam is not around.

When they leave the apartment the space opens up around you. The apartment seems huge. It overwhelms you. You think about dusting a glass table but there is a maid who will do it in a few days if you don't. So instead, you look at the river. A garbage barge floats by. You look closer, watching the water move as the barge presses forward leaving trails of bubbles in its wake. When you are bored, you grab your backpack and a jacket and go out.

At the bookstore you buy a pastry that the clerk tells you is "yummy." He is cute, has a goatee and an earring, and is young enough to be your son. Instead of reading a book or a magazine today you take out a yellow legal pad that you "borrowed" from your job. You make a few notes, write a sentence, then a paragraph, then stop and eat the pastry. You have decided to write down all of the facts you can remember about all of the men you have had sex with. You include the blind dates, set-ups from friends, and near-misses. Then you make a list of those you know who are dead.

o   o   o

You meet Peter and Adam for lunch at a place near the gym. Peter catches you up on his current boy trouble; he has started dating a guy who is twenty-three and an actor, a deadly combination, or so he explains. Peter has always been in love with what he can't have. In a few minutes, the conversation shifts to his last ex-boyfriend.

Adam liked Peter's last ex-boyfriend better than you did. Adam thought the last ex-boyfriend was "hot." One night, in bed, he said to you, "I bet they have great sex." You never liked Peter's last ex-boyfriend. He was always turning the conversation to religion and politics and expressing his opinions, which you didn't always share. The last ex-boyfriend was always trying to pick a fight with you. You think he liked you as little as you liked him.

When Adam goes to the men's room Peter speaks hurriedly. "What's wrong?" he asks. He is worried about you. "You're not falling apart, are you?"

You say you are just adjusting to living with another man for the first time in forty-one years, someone other than a family member or a college roommate. "It's odd being around him all the time, you know. I guess some of the magic wears off."

"It's all about compromise," Peter says, as if he is an expert at living with his lovers. Fifteen years ago was the one and only time Peter lived with a boyfriend. It lasted for six weeks, the boyfriend moving out on Peter's thirtieth birthday. "Are you getting out?" he asks you.

"What do you mean?"

"Doing things without him?"

"I'm fine," you say. "We eat out all the time."

"That's not what I mean," he says.

"I know what you mean."

"I know it's none of my business, but I'm one your oldest friends and I don't like to see you unhappy."

You don't answer him because he forces another question at you, a question you don't have to answer because Adam is walking toward the table the moment Peter asks it: "Would you be happier if you didn't live together?"

o   o   o

Peter's question nags at you all weekend. You spend Saturday night at the theater, a musical that is not very musical with actors who do too much acting. Adam does not enjoy himself and you do not enjoy being with Adam when he is not happy. On Sunday morning, you write down more notes about your past while Adam watches a political show on cable. In the afternoon, you walk to the park, sit on the lawn, and read while Adam watches the rollerbladers, telling you to look up if a shirtless young one rolls by, which today is rare because of the cool air. During a moment when you are walking out of the park you remind yourself how long it has taken you to get to a man you would not walk away from—a live-in relationship. Years and years and years of being gay and single and wanting. A year and a half of dating Adam. It wasn't easy to believe that Adam loved you. It was harder to convince yourself how you could feel about him.

o   o   o

Back at work, on Monday, you are busy with more copying and typing. At several moments you think about calling Adam to check in to see how his day is going. You're busy, though, and forget to do it every moment that you remember to do it or else when you remember it, you are on the phone with somebody else and cannot do it. By five o'clock you feel differently. Peter meant to be helpful, but he doesn't understand the dynamics of relationships, which is why his never work out. You regret wasting so much of your day thinking about what he said. You regret the weekend, too—Saturday was wasted; you had felt vaguely depressed all day and now you realize that Peter was responsible. Not only over what he said about you and your relationship—or what he insinuated— but his presence, a reminder of what can happen to a relationship when two adults who care about each other can't work things out, as Peter and his last ex-boyfriend of six weeks did by deciding to break up.

After work, you walk to the bookstore, order a decaffeinated coffee, sit at a table, and read a travel magazine. You recognize the young man at the cash register from last week as well as the man he is serving. The man at the counter is not much older than the clerk, though he looks like the kind of guy who should be in a music store instead of a bookstore. You watch him pay, shoving the change, including the bills, into his front pocket. He looks out at the tables and carries his tray in your direction.

"Care to share?" he asks and you nod that it is okay for him to join you at the table. You are not certain what is expected of you: if you should try to engage him in conversation or pretend to read your magazine. He solves the problem for you. "What are you reading?" he asks.

You show him the cover of the magazine and he says, "I was in Cancun about two years ago." You almost ask him if it was during a college break though you check yourself and stop, not wanting to sound cynical.

During the next twenty minutes you try to have a conversation while falling into the deep green pools of his eyes. Then you pack up your legal pad and walk with him to his apartment. You think of Adam while you walk along the street, across one neighborhood and into the next, though once you are inside this green-eyed young man's building, inside the apartment and within his bedroom, you are overwhelmed by the sensation of touching a younger man's body. Eventually you untangle from one another, wash up in the bathroom, and get dressed.

"Will you be there again on Friday?" he asks you before you leave.

"I'm not sure yet," you answer. "I'll give you a call."

o   o   o

Adam isn't in the apartment when you get back. You look through the rooms, terrified that he has somehow found out about where you've been. Maybe he followed you to the bookstore. Maybe he noticed you with the young man on the street. What if someone he knows saw you leave together and called him to tell him you are not at home because you are out having an affair? Your nature is too honest to be naturally dishonest. You have clear issues with deception. Yours and his.

You watch TV until you hear his key in the door. You meet him in the hallway, ask him if he wants a drink. His eyes do not meet yours when he says, "How about a martini?" In the kitchen when you are reaching for the shaker, you hear him yell from another room, "Want to order in Chinese?"

o   o   o

The next day you do not show up for work. You get up early and shower, dress, and leave the apartment. The day is gray, chilly, makes you think winter is arriving. For some reason, you did not sleep well. You think it is more from dishonesty than from the chemicals in the Chinese food.

From the bookstore you call your job and tell them you are sick. Then you buy coffee and read a novel at a table. It is about a man in Renaissance London looking for love and at times you become lost in the story of someone else. But most of the time you sit through the day waiting for someone to talk to you—someone, anyone, even the girl who now runs the register. But you spend the day reading, alone, watching the time tick by. When it is late you put the book back on the shelf and walk back to your apartment. Your mind is full of stories you want to write. Love, dates, tricks, affairs, deaths, insomnia, sex. Your life as a novel. When you arrive at the apartment, Adam shuts off his computer, says he wants to try a Mexican restaurant downtown he has heard is good.

Downtown, the food is delicious. You didn't eat lunch at the bookstore and you are starving. You have tamales stuffed with chicken and cheese. Adam has a burrito with black beans and brown rice on the side. After dinner, you walk to a pastry store and Adam orders a slice of chocolate cheese cake. You pretend you are full, satisfied, and content, and you watch him eat his cake. You take a taste of it when he says it is awfully rich. Yes, you agree, it is full of sin. You say, "This is a sinful piece of cake."

o   o   o

155

On Friday, at work, you walk up the stairs instead of taking the elevator. On the third floor you decide you have made a mistake and take the elevator up to the floor where you work. For a moment, walking down the hall to your desk, you think that Adam will be there waiting for you, a scowl on his face, demanding to know why you are trying to wreck your relationship.

He is not there, of course, and the day moves by swiftly, one project overlapping into the next. After work you walk to the bookstore and sit at a table and read the newspaper. After ten minutes or so you begin to think you have made a mistake. You told him the wrong day, the wrong time, the wrong bookstore. Or maybe he changed his mind, decided you're too old, too involved with someone else to pursue. While you are zipping up your newspaper into your backpack you sense someone approaching you in the corner of your vision. When you look up to see who it is you realize you are smiling, the first time you've done so in quite a few days.

o   o   o

Tonight, the restaurant is Japanese, a mistake. Adam says there is a funny taste to his sushi; he can't quite place it, but it doesn't seem right. You say your food tastes fine and you trade with him. He eats off your plate; you eat off his.

By the time you get home you have a headache. Adam says it must have been the fish but you are silently convinced that it is everyone else that is wrong with your life. In the bathroom you throw up in the toilet, wet a washrag with warm water, place it on your forehead, and practice breathing like you were once taught in a yoga class. You hear Adam watching TV in another room; you know you can no longer confront him about his affair because of your own. When you feel better you wash your face and slowly drink a glass of water. During a commercial break, you walk into the room and ask him if he wants a snack. "Sure," he answers. "Let's have some ice cream."

o   o   o

Two days later you are walking toward the bookstore. At a corner, you catch a glimpse of your reflection in a car window, and realize you live in a city full of temptation. Standing there, you think of Adam, off in one direction to an affair, and you, off in the direction to another. The sun is setting against a building and you watch the amber light wash over it, transforming the glass and steel into a golden shrine. Autumn always makes things feel perfect. You wish you could stop time, hit the pause button and live in this moment, this perfect feeling when you think you are happy.

But the days are growing shorter and shorter. Time doesn't stop. In a few more days you will be forty-two. Winter is only steps away. So you keep walking and notice you are hungry. Yes, you think, you are ready to eat.

What You Save

This is how it happens. You walk into the Atlantic next to your boyfriend. It is a week after the hurricane has passed safely around the island. The waves are small, gentle hills. It is August and the water is warm. You say, it's so much different than last week when you tried to swim. He says he's glad the water is warmer this week. You wade out further until the water is up to your stomach. You twist your back to breach the slow, cresting waves. You feel the undertow tug at your feet as the water recedes, grains of sand shifting beneath your toes. Above you the sky is a cloudless blue. It is a perfect day. You squint as you look southward, against the glimmering reflection of the sun spots against water. To your north, a man is diving into the breaking surf; behind him, another couple of men are inching into the water. You wade out to a point where the waves are breaking behind you. You are in water up to your neck, your body rising as the ocean swells, the sensation like being in a rocking tub. Your boyfriend joins you. You say you heard a guy drowned out here last week because the water was so angry. He says he liked the water better then; the waves were more fun. The rocking motion pulls you further out from shore. You tread in the water, mentioning to your boyfriend that the man in the silver swimsuit he was admiring on the beach is now in the water, too.

"We're out too far," your boyfriend says. You hear the worry in his voice. You look at him and see his expression has changed. His eyes are wide. His mouth is open. He is not smiling. His jaw is tense. "My feet don't touch ground."

You think he is joking. You think he is faking being scared. He swivels his head back and forth; his jaw bobs up and down. As you tread water, looking at the calm surf breaking around you, you can no longer feel the undertow, but the motion of the sea is pulling you further away from shore.

It reminds you of a scene in a movie. Or a badly acted TV series. Your boyfriend fakes his drowning for laughs. Or maybe for sympathy. Then something makes you realize he is not faking at all. He is in trouble. You smile at him and say calmly, "We're not in trouble."

He goes under, just like in the movie, and he comes up for air, his eyes glazed with terror. You swim over to him. You touch his arm. "We're okay," you say. "Just tread water, Adam." The thought rushes across your mind that he doesn't know how to swim. But then you remember he does laps in the pool every weekend to try to keep the extra pounds off. His panic rises and he holds on to you and you feel his weight pulling you under.

Your feet are treading fiercely now in order not to let him push you under, as though you were riding a stationary bike at the gym and had cranked up the resistance level. You say, "Adam, just swim toward shore. We'll make it."

He starts swimming but you sense the panic in his body. You say his name again, louder, so he will hear it and understand it. "Adam, catch the wave. Ride the wave in."

You are swimming behind him. You look around; there are two other men swimming close by, only feet away. It's inconceivable to you that someone could drown when someone else was so close by. And on a day like today. Calm, blue water. You lift your head further out of the water, like a turtle nosing out of his shell. You yell to the other men, "Help." It sounds weak and surreal. You try it louder. It sounds like a false alarm to you. Like you are joking about needing help. Like a ploy to pick one of them up. You feel embarrassed and silly. You lift your hand up and wave at the other men, your feet pumping wildly underwater.

Finally, one man looks at you. You wave to him to help pull

your boyfriend in. He doesn't understand and he waves back to you, as if you are friends. You say, "Help" again and point to your boyfriend, who is still swimming toward shore.

You see Adam reach a wave. He rides it in. Behind him, you're suddenly swelled up into a crest of water and forced underneath the surface. You feel your back twist and your head is a roar of sound. You tumble in the water and a darkness comes over you. In the blackness the thing which pushes you up toward the surface is your worry about Adam. It cannot end like this. This is not how it is supposed to end.

Suddenly you realize you can stand and you are out of the water, gasping for air, turning yourself in the direction where you last saw Adam. You are certain you will not find him. That you will have to search for him beneath the surface. But the man you waved to is helping him stand.

You see Adam make his way toward the beach. The man steps over to you and takes your hand. Your legs are shaking. You smile and thank him quickly and take fast steps through the water to catch up with Adam.

Adam has made it to land and is sitting where the sand and water still meet, not even trying to return to where you have set up your beach chairs.

"Are you okay?" you ask.

His head is between his legs. His back is heaving. He doesn't respond.

"Can I do anything?" you ask. You feel a pain at your elbow and twist your arm toward your eyes. You have scraped the skin somehow. It is red and raw. You feel the muscles in your back twist and relax. Pain shoots around your waist. You sit down beside him.

Adam is balled up in fear. You sense he does not want to be touched. "We made it," you say. "We're okay."

You look out at the waves, imagining the worst-case scenario: You watch Adam drown. You watch his body wash to shore. You watch people gather round, waiting for the ambulance to arrive.

You drive the car back to his house alone. You call his ex-lover. You call his brother in the city, his elderly parents in Massachusetts.

"My stomach hurts," Adam finally says.

This is nothing new. He's okay. His stomach always hurts. He has gastrointestinal problems that make him belch. Specialists have sent him home with prescriptions for relief.

"I swallowed a lot of water."

It is your turn to remain silent, to see if he has anything else to say. You nod and place your hand against his thigh, but the action seems strained. Something has changed here.

He stands and you follow him back to the beach chairs. He wraps himself in his large blue towel. You put on your T-shirt. You want to read the issue of *Vanity Fair* you have brought to the beach, but you can't seem to pick it up off the towel. You look out at the ocean again. Blake, a friend, waves at you from the beach, strides across the sand, air-kisses Adam first, then you. He knows nothing of what has just happened. He launches into a monologue about his new job in London. He talks about his boyfriend, Ken, and the house they own in town and have subleased for the season to another gay couple. You see that Adam's lips are blue, his face drained of the usual reddish tint. You see Adam struggling with his words, telling Blake about the house the two of you are renting this summer in the Northwest Woods.

When Blake leaves a few minutes later, you notice Adam is shaking. His teeth are clenched, as if to prevent them from chattering. "I don't feel well," Adam says. "Can we go?"

You begin packing the towels in the knapsack and folding the chairs. "I'll drive," you say.

He hands you the car keys. This has never happened before. He always objects to your driving. He never relinquishes control. As you struggle with walking through the sand, you say, "Should we go to a doctor?"

"No," he says flatly and you walk silently back to the parking lot like a scolded child. At the car, you wipe the sand off your feet and slip on your shoes. Adam waits in the car while you pop open the trunk and put the chairs inside.

You adjust the seat, start the car, and drive slowly out of the parking lot. Adam looks straight ahead. "I guess my number's not up," he says, when you reach the stop light.

He remains silent the rest of the ride. So do you. At the house he goes upstairs and lies on the bed. You go to the kitchen and pour yourself a drink. As you reach to return the bottle to the shelf you feel the pain in your back again. You take your drink to the outside deck, sitting in a chair beside the umbrella-topped table. You look at the light coming through the bright green leaves of the trees of the wooded property, making them look as if they have been charged with neon. You want to feel relaxed but you can't. You imagine what would have happened if you had drowned saving Adam. He could easily dispense your stuff into a plastic garbage bag; all that you have here are the gifts you have given him: cookbooks, utensils, CDs, beach toys—stuff you care more about than he does.

You listen to the wind moving through the leaves. You have never made the transition from boyfriends to lovers, even though you share an apartment in the city and a weekend house in the country. You know you can be easily replaced. It has happened before. You have always been aware that you are only a temporary fixture at this house—the posters you brought to hang on the walls could last longer than you.

A squirrel scampers across the deck with an acorn in its mouth, up the fence posts of the deck, and then leaps for a tree branch, the limb shaking beneath its weight as it scurries forth. Adam says that you've grown meaner this summer; everything about you is tense. You say it is because your job has become a disappointment. Office politics. Mismanagement. No growth, no encouragement to continue. You want to do something meaningful. Your head is full of stories you want to write but have no energy to complete. Adam doesn't understand that the job exhausts you, that *he* exhausts you. He doesn't understand that when you arrive at the house on the weekend that all you want to do is watch the leaves, listen to the surf, find a way to clear your mind.

You sit and sip at your drink, watching the breeze move the limbs of the trees above you. A pebble travels down the roof and onto the deck, landing between small black chunks of the roof, cracked apart by the sun. Things have been falling apart all summer. You no longer drive out to the country together. He wants to arrive early and leave late, using the excuse that he is retired and you are not. You know it is because he is drifting again. You have gained too much weight. He wants someone younger. A boy toy. You know he is out there looking. He's told you so. But he's not ready to call it quits with you yet. He still wants you here. And you can't say no. Together you are a leaky raft still trying to stay afloat.

Things are no longer repaired. They are ignored though not forgotten. The screen door, fallen off its tracks since May, still sits in a corner of the deck. The umbrella over the table has holes along the spokes, sending a strange pattern of light against your leg. He claims that you are uncommunicative. You reply that he only makes announcements: I am buying a new car. I am joining a new gym. I am going to Palm Springs. But not with you.

Standing up, you feel a sliding sensation as if the deck had been tipped. You set the glass on the table and walk over to the pool. You take your shoes off and set them atop a warped plank of the deck. You dangle your feet into the water. It is much cooler than the ocean. And then there is the money. He has too much. You don't have enough. Rich and poor have never made a good match. This has lasted much longer than anyone—your friends or his—expected, three years together feeling like thirty. You feel like you have been in this relationship forever—without any return on your investment.

You inch your body into the water. You hold your breath as it eases up above your waist. Then you quickly dive headfirst into the water, swimming to the bottom and coming up for air at the last possible moment. His mid-life crisis has helped create yours. When his ex-lover visited in June, you were introduced only as a friend. When you ran into his former co-workers outside the cinema in town, he didn't even bother to introduce you. After all this time, there are no pictures of you together, no favorite songs, no shared souvenirs. You do not celebrate Valentine's Day or anniversaries. Birthdays come and go without meaning. Together you are alone and lonely. Now you must sink or swim.

You swim a few laps but feel another sharp pain at your back. You know something's been twisted too far, but you can't even fathom finding a doctor. You dive underwater again and come up for air, push your arms through a pink inner tube. The water will last longer at this house than you will. It's chemically treated. Never drained. You lie motionless in the water, drifting where the jet flows from the filter send you. You don't even have energy left to swim.

As you float you watch the day change around you. The light shifts lower in the sky. The leaves grow darker. You wonder about what to fix to eat. You wonder if he will want to cancel going to the movies tonight. Apathy settles in around you. You haven't even had the energy this summer to want to meet someone else. Dating seems like a foolish exercise. Life is too many challenges, everything an obstacle that beats you before you can try. You don't have time to clean the apartment, do the grocery shopping, take care of yourself. What energy you maintain is for him. You cook for him, you pamper him, you indulge him, you make love to him even as you watch him drift elsewhere.

You decide you want another drink. You dry yourself off with an oversized towel and walk into the kitchen. You fix another drink. You drink it quickly. You know your drinking is out of control. You pour yourself another anyway, take a sip, and leave the glass on the counter.

You walk upstairs to the bedroom, keeping your steps light so as not to wake him. He is face down on the bed. He never sleeps like this. You wonder what you should do. He is still breathing so you know he is alive. No need to call a doctor. The floor shifts, creaks beneath your weight when you enter the bedroom. He stirs in the bed, turns his head. His eye looks up at you.

You sit on the edge of the bed. You don't know what to say. You want to reassure him that you love him, but the words catch in your throat. You know you've reached the point where you don't expect the sentiment to echo back. "We're here," you say, "and you're okay."

He doesn't respond. There is no sign of surviving. You wish to be out of this, the vain and petty effort to be happy, to pretend you still care.

But then he reaches out his arm and his fingers touch you at your wrist. Even in this emptiness it is the one thing that remains between the two of you. The shared desire to be a part of another person's life.

Your fingers find their way to his, folding themselves into a familiar pattern. You look away from him. He no longer makes you feel alive. You imagine yourself floating in the ocean alone, a lifeless body waiting to be discovered. You wonder if anyone can revive you or if you've already drowned. Perhaps you'll never be recovered. You've drifted too far from shore. Lost, you think. You are lost at sea.

Acknowledgments

For their support of these stories, my thanks and appreciation go to Anne H. Wood, Brian Keesling, Richard Labonté, Daphne Young, Danielle Unis, Neenyah Ostrom, David Olin Tullis, Debra Riggin Waugh, Marti Hohmann, Christopher Bram, Kevin Bentley, Kirk Read, B.A. St. Andrews, Sean Meriwether, Charles Allen Wyman, Andrew McBeth, Michael Huxley, David Groff, Charles Flowers, Hugh Coyle, Will Berger, Aaron Smith, and Wesley Gibson. For their ongoing support of my writing and the press, I would also like to thank Jon Marans, Martin Gould, Larry Dumont, Joel Byrd, Deborah Collins, John Maresca, Andrew Beierle, Kathy Corey, Ellen Herb, Teresa Smith, Hermann Lademann, Ed Iwanicki, Lawrence Schimel, Jay Quinn, David Pratt, Michael Graves, Tom Cardamone, Steve Berman, Vince Liaguno, Wayne Hoffman, Mark Sullivan, Greg Herren, Paul Willis, and Arch Brown. Grateful acknowledgment is made to the New York Foundation for the Arts for its support of these stories and to the memory and the friendship of those lost to AIDS, particularly Kevin Patterson and David Feinberg.

About the Author

Jameson Currier is the author of four novels: *Where the Rainbow Ends*, a Lambda Literary finalist, *The Wolf at the Door, What Comes Around,* and *The Third Buddha*; and four collections of short fiction: *Dancing on the Moon; Desire, Lust, Passion, Sex; Still Dancing: New and Selected Stories;* and *The Haunted Heart and Other Tales,* which was awarded a Black Quill Award. His short fiction has appeared in many literary magazines and Web sites, including *Blithe House Quarterly, Velvet Mafia, Confrontation, Christopher Street,* and the anthologies *Men on Men 5, Best American Gay Fiction 3, Certain Voices, Best Gay Erotica, Best American Erotica, Best Gay Romance, Best Gay Stories, Circa 2000, Rebel Yell, Wilde Stories, Unspeakable Horror, Art from Art,* and *Making Literature Matter.* In 2010 he founded Chelsea Station Editions, an independent press devoted to gay literature, and the following year launched the literary journal *Chelsea Station.*

www.ingramcontent.com/pod-product-compliance
Lightning Source LLC
Chambersburg PA
CBHW071221260626
47162CB00004B/1379